P.6

This
book
belongs
to
Robert Slonem
31 Ivanhoe Place
Valley Strea
N. Y.
11580

"OH, MAH GOODNESS! WHO DONE LEFT IT YEAH?"

The Bobbsey Twins and Baby May   *Frontispiece (Page 33)*

The Bobbsey Twins and Baby May

BY
LAURA LEE HOPE
AUTHOR OF "THE BOBBSEY TWINS SERIES,"

NEW YORK
GROSSET & DUNLAP
PUBLISHERS

Made in the United States of America

CONTENTS

THE BOBBSEY TWINS
AND BABY MAY

CHAPTER I

A RAILROAD SMASH

"Just look at it rain!" exclaimed Nan Bobbsey to her brother Bert, as they were getting their coats, hats and umbrellas from the schoolroom closet.

"Crickity grasshoppers, I should say so!" cried Bert, crowding to the one window in the coatroom, already filled with boys and girls eager to escape from school. "It's bouncing up from the sidewalk something awful!"

"Well, I know one thing," announced Charlie Mason, pushing his face against the windowglass until his nose looked flat. "The rain isn't going to bounce on my umbrella."

"Why not?" asked Bert. "Aren't you going to put your umbrella up in all this storm?"

"Nope!" answered Charlie, with a laugh and a shake of his head.

"Why not?" asked Nan curiously.

" 'Cause I didn't bring an umbrella, that's why!" chuckled the boy.

"You'll get soaked!" said Danny Rugg. "I haven't got a very big umbrella, Charlie, but you can walk under it with me."

"Thanks," murmured Charlie.

"Danny's getting real good, isn't he, Bert?" asked Nan, as these two dark-haired Bobbsey twins made their way out of the coatroom and toward the main hall, which was filled with boys and girls eager to get home.

"Yes, Danny's pretty good now," agreed Bert. "And I'm glad of it. He always used to be fighting and quarreling. Say, Nan, it's raining like cats and dogs!"

"Worse than that!" sighed Nan. "I hope Flossie and Freddie won't get soaked."

"Didn't they bring umbrellas?" Bert wanted to know. "If they didn't—"

"Oh, yes, they brought their little ones. I saw mother call them back and make them take them," replied Nan Bobbsey. "But even a big umbrella isn't much good in this storm. The wind blows terribly! I'm going to wait in the lower hall for Flossie and Freddie."

"All right; I'll wait with you," offered Bert good-naturedly.

As the older Bobbsey twins stood there, watching the other boys and girls pass out, the rain now and then blew in through the open door.

A gust of wind would send the door swinging back after some child had tried to close it, and the water would streak across the floor, leaving little puddles.

"It's a regular flood!" laughed Bert, as he and his sister waited for the smaller twins, who studied in another room, which had not yet been dismissed.

"There'll be a lot of puddles on the way home," remarked Nan.

"Say, do you know what I'm going to do?" asked Bert, as he saw Danny Rugg and Charlie Mason going out arm in arm, the better to fit under one small umbrella.

"What are you going to do?"

"I'm going to take off my shoes and stockings, and I'll wade home!" declared Bert.

"Oh, you are not!" cried Nan.

"Yes, I am!"

"I'll tell mother if you do!"

"Pooh! Won't she see me anyhow, if I wade home? I tell you it's better to take off your shoes and stockings than to step in a lot of puddles and get soaked."

"Well, I'm not going to do that!" said Nan. "It's too cold!"

"I'm going to. I don't care for the cold," decided Bert, and then and there he sat down and took off his shoes and stockings, putting his stockings in his shoes and hanging his shoes around his neck by the laces.

"Now I'm all ready for a washout!" he cried.

"Here come Flossie and Freddie," reported Nan. "Hurry, children," she begged them. "We want to get home before the storm grows any worse."

"Oh, I'm going to take off my shoes and stockings!" cried Freddie, as he saw what Bert had done.

"So'm I!" added Flossie, who always wanted to do what Freddie did.

"No! No!" cried Nan. "You mustn't! There, see what you've started!" she added to Bert. "I knew they'd want to do this when they saw you!"

"Well, I can't help that," chuckled Bert. "Let 'em if they want to, I say!"

"No! No!" insisted Nan, as she saw the younger twins sitting down and beginning to tug at their shoe laces. "You mustn't! Mother wouldn't like you to go barefoot in this cold rain—it isn't summer yet. Keep your shoes on!"

"But Bert has his off, and I want to wade in the puddles!" wailed Flossie.

"So do I!" echoed Freddie. "I want my shoes off!"

"I'll be the ferryman and carry you over the puddles," offered Bert, and this solved the problem, much to Nan's delight.

Flossie and Freddie kept on their shoes and stockings, and followed their older brother and sister out into the storm. They were almost the last to leave the school, on account of the little dispute.

Down pelted the rain so hard that, as Nan

had said, the umbrellas were of little use. The wind blew the wet drops under them. But the children rather enjoyed it, and Flossie and Freddie squealed with delight when Bert carried them across puddles at the gutters, the barefooted boy wading boldly through the muddy water.

"Are you soaked, children?" asked Mrs. Bobbsey, when they reached home. "And Bert—barefooted!"

"It's a good thing I am," said Bert, "else my shoes would be spoiled. I had to carry Flossie and Freddie over a lot of puddles. Their feet aren't so awful wet."

"You poor dears! I ought to have had you take your rubbers as well as your umbrellas," said Mrs. Bobbsey. "I thought we had had enough of April showers."

"Maybe this is the last one, seeing to-day's the last of April," remarked Nan, walking toward the kitchen to put her dripping umbrella in the sink.

"Your feet are soaking wet—I can hear them," said Mrs. Bobbsey.

"Yes, they are a little wet," admitted Nan,

looking down at them. "I jumped over most of the puddles, and Bert lifted me across one big one, but I guess I got a little wet, anyhow."

"A *little* wet! I should say you *did!*" exclaimed Mrs. Bobbsey. "Now all of you put on dry things!"

When this had been done, and the Bobbsey twins, safe and dry, looked out of the window at the pelting rain, they were very glad to be sheltered and in their comfortable home.

"Oh, look at the funny old lady!" exclaimed Freddie, who was kneeling on a chair near a front window. "She looks like Mother Goose!"

"But she hasn't got a goose!" added Flossie.

"She has a green umbrella," returned Freddie. "It's a big one, too. Mother, why don't you get me a big green umbrella like hers?" he asked.

"I'm afraid the wind would blow you away with it," laughed Mrs. Bobbsey, as, with Bert and Nan, she looked out at the person Flossie and Freddie were speaking of. "Poor old lady!" murmured Mrs. Bobbsey.

The old woman making her way up the street amid the storm, carrying on one arm a large, square market basket covered with a black cloth, as if to keep whatever was inside dry from the pelting rain, did, indeed, seem a strange figure.

As she walked along, holding her large, green umbrella over her head, she glanced now and then from beneath it at the houses she passed. She caught sight of the four Bobbsey twins at the window of their home, and halted a minute, gazing intently at them.

"Oh, do you s'pose she's coming here?" gasped Nan.

"No, I think not," replied Mrs. Bobbsey. Then the old woman walked slowly on, still peering curiously at the house.

"Isn't she odd?" murmured Nan to Bert. "I wonder what she has in that basket, and what she is looking for."

"Maybe she sells things," suggested Bert. "Well, I know what I'm going to do if mother won't let me go out and play boat." He had asked to be allowed to do this, but Mrs. Bobbsey had said no.

"What you going to do?" asked Freddie.

"I'm going to make an elevated railroad," declared Bert.

"Oh, can you?" cried Freddie. "And may I help?"

"May I ride on it?" questioned Flossie.

Nan remained at the window, looking at the queer old woman as she vanished down the street in the mist from the rain. Though Nan did not know it, this same old woman was soon to play a strange part in the lives of the Bobbsey twins.

"How you going to make an elevated railroad?" asked Freddie.

"I'll show you," answered Bert. "No, Flossie, you can't ride on it," he added, as his smaller sister again made her request. "It's only the toy railroad put up on some chairs."

"Oh, that'll be fun!" cried Freddie. "I'll help!"

He began dragging chairs away from the dining-room table, while Bert got from the closet, where it was kept, a toy train of cars that ran by electricity on a sectional track. Instead of putting the track together on the floor, as he usually did, Bert had decided to raise it in the air, supporting it on chairs and boards, thus making an elevated railroad.

"Be careful now, children," warned Mrs. Bobbsey, when she saw what they were doing. "Don't get hurt."

"No'm, we won't!" they chorused.

Bert had taken Dinah's two ironing boards, the large one and the small one, and with some other boards and boxes from the cellar and by the use of chairs, had made a place to put together his tracks.

"You can see 'em a lot better when they're up high this way," said Freddie, as the track was nearly completed.

"I wish I could ride on it. I like to ride on elevated railroads," sighed Flossie. "I rided on one when I was in New York once," she added.

"Well, you can't ride on this!" replied Bert. "You'd break it all up if you did. Hand me that curved track, Freddie, and then I guess it's all done."

The last section of track was put in place, Bert connected the battery, set the engine and cars on the rail, turned the switch, and the elevated railroad was in operation.

"Whee, this is fun!" shouted Freddie.

"It's awfully cute!" said Nan.

"Could I give my little celluloid doll a ride?" asked Flossie. "She's so light a fly could carry her on its back, Bert."

"Yes, give the doll a ride," Bert said, and with smiles of delight Flossie set her on top of one of the toy cars.

The Bobbsey twins made up a game to play with the elevated railroad: They pretended they were sending loads of different things one to the other. Bits of paper were oranges and burned matches did very well for bunches of bananas.

"My, it's raining harder than ever!" exclaimed Bert, as he went to the window to look out.

"Do you see the old lady with the green umbrella?" asked Nan.

"No," her brother answered. "She's gone. Hi, Freddie, what you doing?" he asked, as he saw the little fellow crawling under the large ironing board laid across the seats of two chairs.

"I'm playing I'm under the railroad bridge," said Freddie.

"Oh, I'm coming under, too!" cried Flossie, and she crawled to where Freddie sat under the ironing board.

"Be careful!" warned Bert. "Don't jiggle that board or you'll upset the whole railroad! You'd better come out from under there."

He reached to get hold of Freddie's arm to drag him forth. Just then a loud clap of thunder sounded.

"Oh!" screamed Flossie, and she made a dash, tumbling over.

Bang! down came the ironing board, elevated railroad, toy engine, cars and everything, on the heads of the smaller Bobbsey twins. At that moment another terrific clap of thunder fairly shook the house, and Nan cried out in terror and Bert, too, uttered an exclamation of fear.

CHAPTER II

MYSTERIOUS BELLS

"CHILDREN! What has happened?" cried Mrs. Bobbsey, running in from the kitchen where she was helping Dinah get supper. She gave one glance at the collapsed elevated toy railway, saw Flossie and Freddie buried under an overturned chair, the ironing board, the engine and cars and gasped: "Oh, are you hurt?"

Another loud clap of thunder drowned, for a moment, the answering voices of the children. Then from the toy railroad wreck came the faltering cry of Flossie as she said:

"Oh, I got a terrible bang on the head! Oh, dear!"

"You aren't hurt much—you're just frightened!" said Nan, soothingly, as she helped her small sister get out from beneath the ironing board.

"And I got banged on the knee!" exclaimed Freddie.

"Crickity grasshoppers!" exclaimed Bert, as he viewed the tangled mass of what, a moment before, had been a fine-running toy railroad system. "Everything's gone to smash!"

"Oh, it's a wreck! Let's play it's a railroad wreck!" shouted Freddie. "That's what it is—and I'll be a passenger that was hurt, and Flossie can be another passenger, and you must send for the amberlance, an' Nan can be a trained nurse an'—an'—" He had to stop for breath, he was talking so fast.

"We don't need to *pretend* it was a wreck—it sure *is* one!" declared Bert ruefully. "I hope my electric engine isn't smashed!" he added. "Crawl out of there, Freddie, until I take a look!"

"Will I get a shock from the 'lectric battery?" faltered Flossie, as Nan picked her up.

"Yes, Bert, be careful about the electricity, especially in a lightning storm," admonished his mother.

"There's no danger," the older Bobbsey boy insisted. "The wires are broken, I guess.

Who pulled that ironing board down, anyhow?"

"Freddie did," said Flossie.

"I did not! You jiggled me and my head hit it. Anyhow, the thunder knocked it down," insisted Freddie.

"Well, come out of the mess and clear the wreck away," suggested Mrs. Bobbsey. "It's almost time for supper. Daddy will soon be here and—"

A vivid flash of lightning that seemed to fill the room with its glare, followed by a terrific clap of thunder, stopped her from talking.

"Oh, what a terrible storm!" murmured Mrs. Bobbsey.

Into the room came waddling fat old Dinah, the colored cook.

"Am any ob mah honey lambs hurt?" she inquired anxiously.

"No one is hurt," replied Mrs. Bobbsey. "But, oh, such a mess!" She looked at the conglomeration of chairs, ironing boards, boxes and the toy railroad, now scattered over the floor.

"We'll clean it up," said Bert cheerfully.

And while he and Nan are doing this and while
Mrs. Bobbsey is comforting Flossie and Freddie, who were alarmed over the storm, I shall
take just a moment to tell my new readers a
little something about this family.

In the first book of this series, "The Bobbsey
Twins," you learn that Mr. and Mrs. Richard
Bobbsey lived with their two sets of twins in
the eastern city of Lakeport on Lake Metoka,
where Mr. Bobbsey owned a large lumberyard.
Bert and Nan, who had dark hair and eyes,
were several years older than Flossie and Freddie, whose hair was light and whose eyes were
blue.

Bert and Nan and Flossie and Freddie were
fond of fun and good times, and they had
plenty of them in the country, at school, at the
seashore and on trips.   There are various
books telling of the adventures of the Bobbsey
twins in different places, at grandpa's farm,
on the deep blue sea, and out West.   Just before this story opens the Bobbsey twins had
been camping and had had some wonderful
adventures.

"Well, Bert, was anything broken?" asked

his mother, when the "mess," as she called it, of the elevated railroad had been cleared away.

"No, nothing much, Mother," he answered. "One of the cars lost a wheel, but that's always coming off. I guess Sam can fix it." Sam was Dinah's husband, a jolly, stout, colored man-of-all-work about the Bobbsey place.

"I think you'd better wash now and get ready for supper," his mother told him.

"If I could put on my bathing suit and stand out in the rain I wouldn't have to wash—the shower would wash me," Bert said, laughing.

"Oh, could we do that? Could we put on our bathing suits?" begged Freddie.

"Please!" begged Flossie, who was all over her crying spell caused by having been hit on the head when the ironing board fell.

"No, indeed!" laughed Mrs. Bobbsey. "This isn't summer yet. The rain is a cold one. I hope your father doesn't get drenched. But what made your elevated railroad fall, Bert?"

"Oh, I guess Flossie or Freddie moved one of the chairs when they crawled under the ironing board to make believe they were under a bridge," the boy answered.

"I didn't!" asserted Freddie. "It was the thunder!"

"Well, maybe it was," admitted Bert. "It rumbled terribly loud, anyhow."

"Hark!" exclaimed Nan suddenly.

"Oh! is it going to thunder again?" cried Flossie, getting ready to bury her head in Nan's lap.

"No. But I think I heard daddy come in," said the older Bobbsey girl.

"Yes, there he is!" cried Bert, and a moment later Mr. Bobbsey, his face sparkling with rain drops that had blown beneath his umbrella, entered the room.

"All safe and sound?" he asked cheerfully.

"Yes," his wife answered. "But if you had been here a little while ago—"

"Why, what happened?"

"Oh, my elevated railroad was wrecked!" laughed Bert, and by turns the children told of the happening.

"Daddy," began Nan a little later, as they sat at the supper table, the storm having quieted somewhat. "Daddy—"

"Yes, Nan?" he answered. "What is it?"

"Did you see a funny old lady with a green umbrella out in the storm?"

"What's this—a riddle?" and Mr. Bobbsey smiled.

"Oh, no! We all saw her!" cried Freddie.

"An' she had a big basket!" added Flossie.

Mr. Bobbsey looked at his wife, to ask what it was all about, and she told briefly about the strange woman passing the house in the storm, carrying the big basket, which seemed to be heavy.

"No, I didn't see her," said Mr. Bobbsey. "It's hard to see anything in this storm," he added. "Is my rubber coat here at the house?" he asked his wife.

"Why?" she wanted to know, looking quickly at him. "You aren't going out again to-night, are you?"

"I'm afraid I'll have to," he replied. "The river is rising with so much rain, and I have men moving back some of the lumber so it won't be washed away. But I'll not be gone longer than I can help."

The Bobbsey twins were disappointed that their father could not remain indoors with them and tell stories this stormy night.   But, as he explained, it was needful that he look after his lumber, many great piles of which were on the very brink of the river that flowed into Lake Metoka.

"I started men moving back some of the piles before I left to come home to supper," he said.   "I want to go back and find out how much more is left."

"Could I come with you?" Bert begged.

"No, I'm afraid not, little man," his father answered.   "You couldn't do anything in the darkness, and you'd only be in the way."

"Could I go down to-morrow?"

"Maybe.   I'll see about it," promised Mr. Bobbsey.   He put on his big rubber coat and went out into the storm after supper.

The thunder and lightning seemed to have passed over, but it was still raining hard.   Mrs. Bobbsey let the younger twins stay up a bit later than usual, but at last their nodding heads showed her it was time they went to bed.   Bert and Nan soon followed and Mrs. Bobbsey sat down to read until her husband should return.

The wind howled mournfully through the

trees, dashing the rain against the windows, and, more than once, Mrs. Bobbsey looked up and shivered a little as she thought of her husband out in the storm, trying to save his lumber from being washed away.

"That poor old woman, too," mused Mrs. Bobbsey, as she thought of the one with the green umbrella. "She looked friendless and forlorn I hope she finds shelter for the night."

She kept on with her reading. Presently there was a rumble of thunder, not so loud, however, but that Mrs. Bobbsey heard the ringing of the front doorbell at the same time.

"I wonder who that is at this time of night, and out in all this storm," she said to herself, as she arose and walked through the front hall. Before she reached the door she heard the patter of bare feet in the upper hall.

"Mother, did you hear the bell ring?" asked Freddie.

"I heard it! I haven't been asleep yet," called Flossie. "Is that daddy come home? I want to kiss him!"

"No, it can't be your father—he has a key," said Mrs. Bobbsey. "Go back to bed this instant, children! You'll catch cold in your nighties! Go back to bed!"

Flossie and Freddie did so, though they did not want to. Mrs. Bobbsey went to the front door. There was an electric lamp outside, which she could light by pushing a button within the hall. This she did and glanced out before opening the door.

But, to her surprise, she saw no one standing on the steps. The rain was running down the glass in little streams, but no one could be seen.

"That's strange," mused Mrs. Bobbsey. "I'm sure I heard the bell ring—and so did the children. Perhaps it was some one who made a mistake and got the wrong house, and after they saw the number they walked away. My, how it rains!"

She went back to her reading. Again came the distant rumble of thunder, following a flash of lightning. And, again, the doorbell tinkled.

"That must be some one!" exclaimed Mrs. Bobbsey, and, she said afterward, she had a "queer feeling" as she again arose and went to the door.

Before she had a chance to switch on the light and look out she once more heard the patter of bare feet in the upper hall.

"Flossie—Freddie—you mustn't get out of bed again!" she called up the stairs.

"This isn't Flossie or Freddie—it's me," said Bert, in a low voice. "I mean it's I," he added, as he recollected that his teacher had corrected him for saying that in class. "Who's ringing the bell, Mother?" he asked.

"That's just what I'm going to find out," answered Mrs. Bobbsey. But when, once more, she looked out on the rain-swept porch she saw no one.

"This is certainly queer!" she exclaimed. "Did you hear the bell, Bert?"

"Yes, Mother, I sure did. I thought it was dad."

"But there is no one here," said Mrs. Bobbsey. "Not a soul!"

"Oh, well, maybe the lightning rang the bell," said Bert.

"Does lightning ever do such things?" Mrs. Bobbsey wanted to know.

"Yes," answered Bert. "We had a lesson

on electricity in class the other day—not much, just a little one—and teacher said it did funny things. I guess it could ring a doorbell without anybody being near."

"Well, perhaps it could," admitted Mrs. Bobbsey. "Certainly no one is here. Better get back to bed, Bert."

"I will, Mother!"

Just then a noise was heard at the back door.

CHAPTER III

BABY MAY

BERT BOBBSEY did not go back to bed right away. Instead, he remained in the upper hall, listening.

"Did you hear that, Mother?" he asked, in a low voice.

"You mean that noise at the back door?"

"Yes. I wonder—"

Nan came tiptoeing out of her room.

"What is it?" she whispered. "What is the bell ringing for, and—"

"Hush!" cautioned Bert.

Then their fears came to a sudden end, for the voice of Mr. Bobbsey was heard in the kitchen asking:

"Where are you, Mary? I forgot my front-door key, and came in the back way."

"I didn't know the back door was open," remarked Mrs. Bobbsey, while Bert, no longer worried, said to Nan:

"It's all right. It's dad. I'm going back to bed."

"Oh," said Nan. "All right!"

The two older Bobbsey twins went to their rooms. Flossie and Freddie had gone back to their beds and were now slumbering peacefully, lulled by the patter of rain drops.

"How did you get in the back door if it was locked?" asked Mrs. Bobbsey of her husband, as he took off his dripping rubber coat.

"I always leave an extra back-door key out over the side window ledge," he answered, "so if I forget my latch key I can get in. That's what I did to-night. But what were you doing in the front hall?" he asked.

"The front doorbell rang," his wife replied. "Was it you ringing it?" she went on quickly.

"I ring the front doorbell? No," Mr. Bobbsey answered. "I thought you might be asleep and I didn't want to disturb you. So when I felt in my pocket and found I hadn't my key—on account of changing my wet trousers for dry ones before supper—I just went to the back door and let myself in."

"It's very strange," said Mrs. Bobbsey, lis-

tening to make sure that none of the twins was
stirring upstairs.

"What is strange?"

"The way the front doorbell rang. Twice!
And each time I looked out I saw no one. If
you didn't ring it, who did?"

"Perhaps you heard something rattling because of the heavy thunder," suggested Mr.
Bobbsey. "The knives and forks in the pan-
try, maybe."

"No, it was the bell," his wife insisted.
"The children heard it upstairs and came out in
their nighties."

"Um!" mused Mr. Bobbsey. "I'll take a
look out myself. It couldn't be any boys playing pranks on a night like this, could it?"

"Hardly, I should think," his wife said.
"But the bell certainly rang."

Mr. Bobbsey looked through the glass of the
door—he did not open it because the rain would
have blown in—but he came out of the hall,
as his wife had done, without having seen any
one.

"No one there," he said.

"Could the lightning have made the bell

ring? You know it's an electric bell," suggested Mrs. Bobbsey. "Bert said it might do it."

"Perhaps," admitted her husband. "I'll take a look at the bell in the morning. It may be that it is so sensitive that the least jar of thunder will make it ring."

"Did you save the lumber?" his wife asked.

"All but a few planks that got away from us. The river and lake are very high. We've had a lot of rain this spring. Now I think I'll eat something and go to bed. Looks as if the rain would keep up into May."

"That's right," agreed the twins' mother. "To-morrow is the first of May, isn't it?"

Her husband nodded as he sat down to a lunch she made ready for him.

It was still raining when Mr. and Mrs. Bobbsey went to bed. But it stopped some time during the night, and when the Bobbsey twins awakened in the morning the sun was shining bright and warm.

"Hurray!" cried Bert, as he looked from his window. "It's cleared off!"

"And there's a big lake in the back lot!"

shouted Freddie. "I can see it from my window."

"We'll sail boats there after school," decided Bert, as he began to dress.

"Maybe we can make a raft and ride on it," proposed Freddie.

"May I have a ride?" begged Flossie. "You wouldn't let me ride on the elevated railroad. Will you let me ride on the raft?"

"It isn't made yet!" laughed Bert. "We'll see about it after school."

"It's going to be a lovely day after the rain," said Nan, as she went downstairs.

"Come, children, get your breakfast and be ready for school," called Mrs. Bobbsey. "I guess you won't need to take umbrellas to-day," she added, with a laugh. "I never saw the sun so bright."

"This will soon dry up the puddles," observed Mr. Bobbsey.

"I hope it doesn't dry 'em all up," ventured Bert. "We want to have some fun in the back lots." Near the Bobbsey home were vacant lots that sometimes filled with rain water and became miniature lakes.

As Nan sat down to breakfast she suddenly looked up and exclaimed:

"Hark!"

"What's the matter?" mumbled Bert, his mouth half full of bread. "Do you think it's thundering again?"

"No! But I thought I heard a cat crying." answered Nan. "Listen!"

They all kept quiet.

Then, faintly, came a little wailing cry.

"Oh, it's a kittie!" exclaimed Flossie. "It's a kittie on the back steps! I'm going to get it!"

She began to get down from her chair.

"That cry came from the front door," said Bert.

"I think so," agreed his father.

"It does sound like a cat," said Mrs. Bobbsey. "Perhaps some one's pet wandered away in the storm last night. But I don't believe it rang the doorbell," she added, with a faint smile.

"No, that was the lightning," insisted Bert.

Nan had hurried to the front of the house. They heard her open the door, and the next moment she uttered a startled cry—almost a cry of alarm.

"What is it?" called Mrs. Bobbsey. "What is it, Nan?"

"Oh, Mother, come quick!" exclaimed Nan. "There's a basket here! A basket—and it has—it has a baby in it! Oh, a little baby!"

The other Bobbsey twins hurried to the front door, followed by their father and mother. They saw Nan bending over a large, square, market basket that rested in the shelter of the doorway, off to one side.

Nan had folded back the heavy cloth cover of the basket. And there, nestled in a warm blanket and looking up at the Bobbseys, was a dear, sweet, cute, little baby, about a year old. It had blue eyes, golden curls, and as it kicked its tiny feet and moved its tiny hands it smiled up at the faces bending over it.

"Oh, my goodness! A baby! A darling baby!" gasped Mrs. Bobbsey.

"Whose is it?" asked Mr. Bobbsey. "Some one must have lost it!"

"They don't *lose* babies!" declared his wife. "It was *left* here!"

"Left here!   On purpose, do you mean?" cried her husband.

Mrs. Bobbsey nodded her head solemnly. Nan had stooped over and was lifting the tiny creature from its nest in the basket.

"Oh, Mother! may we keep it?" begged Flossie.

"Is it a boy or a girl?" demanded Freddie. "If it's a boy, keep it!"

"Bring it in, Nan," said Mrs. Bobbsey. "The poor little dear! It must be almost perished with the cold—and hungry, too! Tell Dinah to warm some milk.   Oh, what a darling child!"

She leaned over and kissed the soft, roselike cheek as the baby nestled in the warm blankets on Nan's arm.

"Hum! A *baby!* I thought it was going to be a *cat!*" murmured Bert, as he picked up the basket.   "Say!" he cried suddenly.   "Look here! I know this basket!"

"You do?" exclaimed his father, with much interest.

"Yes. Look, Nan! It's the basket the queer

old lady with the green umbrella was carrying in the storm yesterday afternoon."

"So it is," agreed Nan. "Oh, Mother! what does it mean?"

"I don't know," was the answer, "except that it seems to mean some one has abandoned this baby. Oh, it's so sweet—a regular doll! Dinah, hurry with that warm milk!"

"Yes'm! Ah's a hurryin, as fast as Ah kin! Oh, fo' de landest sakes! A honey lamb baby! Oh, mah goodness! who done left it yeah?"

"That's what we don't know, Dinah. Nan found it on the steps."

"I thought it was a kitten," said Nan, as she gave the baby to her mother.

"Has it got a name?" asked Freddie.

"Of course not—at least, it probably has, but we don't know it," said his mother. "Oh, you sweet baby!" and she cuddled it to her breast.

"This must be looked into," said Mr. Bobbsey. "Take good care of that basket and everything in it. It's an abandoned baby, all right. And are you sure this basket was the one the strange old lady had?"

"Sure," declared Bert.

"And she had a green umbrella and a faded shawl," added Nan.

"Hum! The police ought to be able to trace her through that description," said Mr. Bobbsey.

"Are you going to have the baby arrested?" demanded Flossie. "I think that's mean!" and she looked sharply at her father.

"Oh, no; of course not, my dear!" said Mrs. Bobbsey. "Daddy means the police must try to find to whom the baby belongs. I can't imagine how any mother could desert it, though. Oh, you little darling!" she murmured, as the baby smiled up at her. "It's a dear little girl," she added.

"Then I know a good name for her," said Bert.

"What?" asked Nan.

"Baby May," replied her brother. "Yesterday was the last of April. To-day is the first of May, so May will be a good name."

"Yes," returned Mrs. Bobbsey, "I should say it would. And Baby May you shall be called until we find out your real name. Now, Dinah, is that milk warm?"

"Yes'm, Ah's comin' wif it! Mah good stars, to t'ink ob a baby like dat ringin' de bell in de middle ob de night! Mah lan'!"

"This baby didn't ring the bell," said Bert.

"Who did den?" demanded the fat, black cook. "Who did den, Ah axes yo', Bert Bobbsey! Who did?"

CHAPTER IV

WHAT THE POLICE FOUND

DINAH's question brought back to the minds of all the Bobbseys, including the smaller pair of twins, the things that had happened in the storm during the night.

"That's right!" exclaimed Bert, snapping his fingers, "this baby couldn't have rung our bell, and yet the bell certainly did ring!"

"I heard it!" said Flossie.

"So did I," added Freddie.

"And we first thought that it was daddy," remarked Nan.

"I think I begin to see what happened," Mr. Bobbsey said. "Bert, you were wrong in thinking the lightning rang the bell."

"I guess I was," Bert admitted. "It was the old lady with the green umbrella and the faded shawl who carried the basket with this baby in it."

36

"Oh, Mother!" gasped Nan. "Do you think she had the baby in the basket all the while—in the rain—while she was going past our house in the afternoon? Do you think so?"

"I do," answered Mrs. Bobbsey.

"And the queer old woman rang our bell," went on Mr. Bobbsey. "She must have seen you children at the window when she passed earlier in the afternoon. She had made up her mind to abandon the baby—that is, leave it on some doorstep—and when she saw children here she must have said to herself that there was a kind mother here."

"And there is!" cried Bert, looking lovingly at his mother. "The best in the world!"

"Thank you, dear," murmured Mrs. Bobbsey softly, as she cuddled Baby May and fed her warm milk.

"So," went on Mr. Bobbsey, "when the queer old woman with the green umbrella saw there were children here, she waited until it was dark enough for her to leave the baby in the basket and then she hurried away. That's what she did. She put the baby on the steps, rang the bell, and ran away."

"That's the reason I didn't see any one when I looked through the glass door," remarked Mrs. Bobbsey. "The old lady was gone."

"Didn't you see the baby in the basket, either?" asked Flossie, putting her littlest finger softly on the roselike cheek of Baby May.

"No, dear, I didn't see the basket," Mrs. Bobbsey answered. "It was off to one side, sheltered from the rain."

"The old lady took good care of the baby, I'll say that, even if she did desert her," resumed Mr. Bobbsey. "After she had rung the bell the first time, she watched, and when she saw that you didn't open the door, she rang it a second time. Then she must have gone away, feeling sure you would come and take the baby in."

"But we didn't!" exclaimed Mrs. Bobbsey. "The poor little dear was out in the rain all night!"

"But she was warmly wrapped up," Mr. Bobbsey said. "And she must have been well fed, for she didn't cry."

"If she did, we didn't hear her," his wife remarked.

"But I'm glad we found Baby May; aren't you, Mother?" asked Nan.

Mrs. Bobbsey looked at her husband and the two exchanged strange glances, though they could not help smiling. Mrs. Bobbsey was already bringing up two sets of twins, and perhaps she did not care to start in with a strange, new baby.

But no woman could help loving sweet Baby May, and the manner in which Mrs. Bobbsey leaned over and kissed the soft cheek showed how tender was her heart.

"Is that all the breakfast she's going to have?" asked Freddie, as he saw the infant turn away from the milk. "I want a lot more than that! I'm hungry! I got to go to school!"

"So have I!" echoed Flossie.

"My gracious, that's so! I almost forgot I had to go to the office!" exclaimed Mr. Bobbsey. "And all the work I've got to do on account of the flood! Come, children, hurry with your breakfasts—but don't eat too fast—and then skip off to school. Your mother will know what to do with the baby."

"You're going to keep her, aren't you, Mother? You're going to keep Baby May, surely!" exclaimed Nan, as she went back to the table.

"We'll see about it," Mrs. Bobbsey answered. "Of course we couldn't keep the baby away from her real father and mother."

"No, of course not," slowly agreed Nan. "But that old woman wasn't her mother, or she wouldn't have left her on our doorstep, would she?"

"I don't believe so," said Mr. Bobbsey.

"She was a kidnapper! That's what she was!" declared Bert.

"Maybe she was a gypsy," suggested Freddie.

"No, I hardly think that," said Daddy Bobbsey. "From what you told me of her, I wouldn'+ say she was a gypsy, and kidnappers don't usually leave the children they take. I don't know just what to think."

"We'll have to notify the police, of course," said Mrs. Bobbsey, in a whisper, for Baby May was now asleep and had been put to bed in a cradle that Dinah brought down from the attic—the cradle Flossie and Freddie had once cuddled in.

"The police! Are you going to have her arrested?" cried Freddie.

"Hush! Not so loud! You'll waken her!" warned his mother, holding up a finger.

"What you going to tell the police for, Daddy?" asked Flossie, in a whisper.

"Because it is the right thing to do," said Mr. Bobbsey. "This baby may have been stolen by this strange old woman. In that case Baby May's father and mother will be wild with grief until they get her back. I must find out from the police if there is any alarm over a kidnapped child. I'll do it before I go to the office."

"Please do it before we go to school," begged Nan. "I want to tell the girls all about Baby May."

Mr. Bobbsey looked at the clock. There was still twenty minutes before the children need start for school, and he could do considerable telephoning in that time. So he called up police headquarters and made a report of the baby being found on his steps.

"Have you any alarm of a child having been kidnapped anywhere around here?" asked Mr. Bobbsey.

"No," answered the officer at police headquarters. "But if we hear of any we'll let you know."

"Have any of your men seen about the town this strange old woman with a green umbrella and a faded shawl?" asked ⸺ Bobbsey, and the twins and Mrs. Bobbsey waited anxiously for the reply. As they could not hear what was said by the police officer, Mr. Bobbsey told them.

"He says none of his men reported seeing the old lady," Mr. Bobbsey retailed. "But he'll inquire of the officers at the railroad station. They'll call me up in a few minutes."

Mr. Bobbsey put the telephone receiver back on the hook and waited. Soon the bell rang, and when the father of the Bobbsey twins had listened a while he turned to his family and said:

"The old lady came in on the train early yesterday morning. The officer at the station remembers seeing her."

"Did she have the basket with the baby in it?" asked Nan.

"She had the covered basket, but the policeman didn't see what was in it," answered Mr. Bobbsey.

"Do they know anything more about her?" Mrs. Bobbsey wanted to know.

"Not much except that she acted rather strangely," was the reply. "She did not seem to know where she wanted to go, and when the officer asked her if he could help her she just shook her head and wandered off."

"Did she tell her name?" Bert inquired.

"The policeman at the railroad station says she mumbled a name something like 'Washington'; but he isn't quite sure about that," Mr. Bobbsey reported.

"Then we could call the baby May Washington," mused Nan.

"Yes, we could," her mother said. "Is that all the police found out?" she inquired of her husband.

"That is all," he said. "They are going to try, however, to find the strange old lady and ask her why she deserted the baby. But we'll have to wait."

"And you children will have to go to school!" exclaimed Mrs. Bobbsey, glancing at the clock.

"But you'll keep Baby May Washington until we come home, won't you, Mother?" pleaded Nan.

"Please do!" begged Flossie.

"I'll see," murmured Mrs. Bobbsey, as the twins hurried on to school, and Freddie said to Bert:

"I'd like her better if she was a boy baby."

CHAPTER V

NAN WHISPERS IN SCHOOL

"WELL, Richard, what do you think of the latest member of the family?" asked Mrs. Bobbsey.

"She's a dear, sweet little thing, but—"

Mr. Bobbsey did not finish what he started to say. He and his wife were bending over and looking at the sleeping baby—May Washington, as she had been hastily named. The Bobbsey twins had gone to school and the house was quiet—just the place for a sleeping baby.

"I can't understand how any mother would leave such a little, helpless baby like this out in a storm all night," went on Mr. Bobbsey, as he prepared to go down to his lumberyard.

"Perhaps it wasn't the mother," said Mrs. Bobbsey. "Certainly that woman seemed too old to be the mother of a little baby like this."

45

"I don't believe she was the mother," declared Mr. Bobbsey, looking for his hat.

"Do you think she was the kidnapper?"

"I don't know what to think. I'll have another talk with the police to-day. You can't do very much over the telephone, but I wanted to satisfy the children a little. Yes, I'll inquire further."

"And what will we do with her—with Baby May, I mean—if the police can't find out to whom she belongs?" asked Mrs. Bobbsey.

"Well—" Mr. Bobbsey turned his hat around several times and looked inside it as if, there, he might find an answer to the puzzling riddle.

"Well?" asked his wife, with a smile, as she waited.

"Um! Well, if we can't find out where she belongs, I suppose the police will have to take her, and—"

"The police!" exclaimed Mrs. Bobbsey, and then she clapped her hand over her mouth, for she had, in her excitement, spoken so loudly that she was afraid of waking the infant. "Why, Richard Bobbsey!" she went on in a whisper, "you wouldn't turn a helpless little baby like May over to a lot of men police, would you?"

"Well, of course I didn't mean exactly that," he murmured. "But we can't keep her—she belongs to some one else—and the police will know what to do with her. You always give abandoned babies to the police."

"Oh, do you?" asked his wife, with a smile. "Well, this is the first time I ever saw or had an abandoned baby, so I don't know. And what do the police do with the babies?" she asked. "Lock them in an iron cell?"

"Of course not!" exclaimed Mr. Bobbsey. "They send them to a nursing home, a founding asylum, an orphanage—or somewhere. I don't know exactly myself; but the police know what to do."

"Yes, I suppose so," agreed his wife, with a smile. "But it seems hard to turn a sweet little baby like this over to a lot of men, even if they are kind, to have them take her to an orphan asylum."

"Oh, they have police women, or matrons,

or something like that to look after kidnapped babies," said Mr. Bobbsey.

"Richard Bobbsey," his wife whispered, as she followed him to the front door, "I don't believe there's a single police woman, or matron, in Lakeport!"

"Well, they'll have to get one then. Anyhow, we can't keep the baby. She will have to go to some asylum."

"Yes, I suppose so," and Mrs. Bobbsey sighed. "It seems strange that she should be left with us, when there are good neighbors on either side of us."

"Neighbors without children—yes," laughed Mr. Bobbsey. "That old woman with the green umbrella knew what she was about when she left her basket here. She saw our twins at the window and she knew we were the kind to look after a baby. But, as you say, we can't keep her, of course."

"No, I suppose not," and Mrs. Bobbsey went back to look at the sleeping baby while her husband hurried on to his lumber office. "Poor, lonely little dear!" she murmured, bending over Baby May. "I wonder who your mother is!"

Big, fat, jolly, black Dinah tiptoed in.

"Am de honey lamb sleepin'?" she whispered. "Does she want any mo' hot milk?"

"Not yet, Dinah," Mrs. Bobbsey said. "But you might have some ready for her when she awakens. And bake a potato for her, Dinah. She's too old to live entirely on milk. She must be about a year old, I should say."

"Ain't she sweet!" whispered Dinah, touching gently with her fat black finger the rose-petal cheek of sleeping May. "Ah jes' lubs dat honey lamb!"

"I should think any one would love her," returned Mrs. Bobbsey, fondly.

"Yo' t'inks she am about a yeah old? She suttenly am very small."

"I should say about a year, Dinah. But, of course, I am not at all sure. Babies are sometimes deceiving when it comes to age. Some grow much faster than others."

"Don't see how nobody could go off an leab dat chile alone on de doahstep," muttered the colored cook, as she waddled back to the kitchen.

Mr. Bobbsey reached his office, and finding that the storm had not done as much damage to his lumberyard as he had feared, went to the police to learn more, if he could, about the abandoned baby. He talked first with the officer at the railr_ _ station.

"What train did the old lady with the basket come in on?" the _ _her of the Bobbsey twins asked.

"That I couldn't say," answered Jim Tully, the policeman at the station. "Two trains got in at the same time, and I don't know which one she got off from. I could ask the conductors, though."

"I wish you would," said Mr. Bobbsey. "I'd like to get this baby back to her father and mother. They must be wild about losing her."

"I should say so!" agreed Mr. Tully. "I've got six of my own, and I know my wife and I'd be crazy if one of 'em was missing over night. I'll see what I can find out for you."

"And if you can't find out anything,"

went on Mr. Bobbsey, "what are we to do with this baby?"

"Hum!" mused Mr. Tully. "That I don't know. I'll have to ask the chief. You don't want to keep it, I s'pose?" he asked.

"Why—er—I don't know. We hardly thought of that," said Mr. Bobbsey.

"No, of course not. Being a strange baby, your wife wouldn't want to be bothered. Well, I'll see what I can find out for you. But I took particular notice of the old lady. I saw the basket was big and pretty heavy for her, and I offered to help her carry it to the waiting room after she got off the train. But she wouldn't let me—she drew away."

"She was afraid you'd find out there was a baby in the basket, I suppose," suggested Mr. Bobbsey.

"I reckon so," agreed the officer. "I'll see the chief and ask what you'd better do with the child if we can't locate the old lady. You say she passed your house?"

"Yes, twice, my wife said. I'll go down and see the chief myself. I've got to do something about the baby."

Mr. Bobbsey had his talk with the chief of the Lakeport police. Meanwhile, because of Mr. Bobbsey's earlier telephone message, inquiries had been made of other officers, and a search started for the strange old woman, but she could not be found.

"You see, Mr. Bobbsey," said Chief Gallagher at the town hall, "we haven't any matron or police woman here, and if you turn the baby over to us I'll have to send to Hilldale for a woman to look after her. They have a matron at Hilldale."

"Well, we can keep the baby for a day or so," said Mr. Bobbsey. "My wife seems rather fond of her. I guess I'd better put an advertisement in the papers—what do you think?"

"I would," agreed the chief. "That's right—advertise for the baby's father and mother. And I'll be on the lookout for any news. If the child was stolen away from some other city we'll hear about it. There'll be a piece in the papers. You just wait a few days."

The Bobbsey twins, talking of the big storm

and the new baby, reached school. Before entering the yard where the other children were at play, Bert said:

"Now, Flossie and Freddie, don't say anything about the baby."

"Why not?" Flossie asked. "I was going to tell Mary Holmes. She's got a baby at her house an' she's always saying we haven't any. Now I can tell her we *have!*"

"No, don't say anything about it," warned Bert. "Mother and daddy might not like it. Wait until we find out who the baby belongs to. Now mind, Flossie and Freddie, don't tell any of your friends about the baby."

"Oh, all right," agreed Flossie, for her mother had told her she must do as Bert said while at school.

"I don't care about a girl baby," murmured Freddie. "If she was a boy, so I could have a brother littler'n what I am, I'd like it all right."

"Well, don't say anything," warned Bert. He turned to say the same thing to Nan, but she had walked on ahead to talk with some of her girl chums, and Bert did not bother to follow. "I guess Nan won't say anything, anyhow," he thought.

But he little knew Nan Bobbsey. She was just bursting with the news and longing to whisper it to her best chum, Nellie Parks, who sat with her.

But the Bobbsey twins had been delayed a little that morning, because of finding the baby, and the last bell rang as they reached the school yard. So Nan had to hurry into her classroom without a chance to tell Nellie the news.

The morning exercises were held. The children sang a hymn and then took part in the beautiful ceremony of saluting the flag. Then the different classes, including the one Flossie and Freddie were in, marched from the assembly room and the day's lessons began.

It was a beautiful day, warm and sunny, after the cold April rain—a perfect May day, so Nan thought, as she looked from the schoolroom window.

And this—thinking of a May day—made her remember the little baby at home.

Hardly aware of what she was doing, Nan turned to Nellie and whispered:

"Oh, I've got the greatest news for you! You'll never guess what we have at our house!"

"A new piano!" guessed Nellie, in a whisper.

"No! It's a *baby!*" and Nan whispered so shrilly that the teacher heard her and looked up in surprise.

"Nan Bobbsey! were you whispering?" asked Miss Riker.

"Ye—yes—yes'm—I—I was!" faltered Nan, realizing, too late, what she had done.

"What were you saying?" Miss Riker asked, not unkindly. "Was it about the lesson, Nan?"

"No'm. It was about—about the new baby at our house!"

"Oh, a new baby! That's lovely!" and Miss Riker smiled. "But you shouldn't whisper about it in school, Nan. When did the baby come?"

"Last night—in the rain. It was left on our doorstep in a basket—and I heard it cry.

I thought it was a kitten—and it was a baby!"

There was a gasp of surprise from all the pupils in the room.

"Nan Bobbsey!" exclaimed Miss Riker, rather sternly, "are you making up a fairy story?"

"Oh, no!" exclaimed Nan. "It's all true!" And she was allowed to tell the class what had happened. It was so unusual that Miss Riker forgot all about lessons, for which the boys and girls were very glad. And so the story of the abandoned baby was known all over the school at recess.

CHAPTER VI

THE RUNAWAY

"SAY, this is a fine thing!" exclaimed Bert Bobbsey, walking up to his sister Nan when recess was almost over.

"What's a fine thing?" Nan wanted to know.

"Why, everybody knows about the baby at our house! I told Flossie and Freddie not to tell, and you let it out right in class!"

"Well, I couldn't help it!"

"You could so!"

"I couldn't! I whispered about it to Nellie and teacher heard me whisper and she asked me and I had to tell. I didn't know I shouldn't!"

"Gosh! That's just like a girl—telling everything! What do you know about that!" and Bert turned to Danny Rugg.

"Sure! That's right! Girls can't keep a secret!" declared Danny.

"We can so—if we want to!" exclaimed Nan. "Anyhow, it would have to be known about the baby when father told the police."

"Oh—all right—there's no use worrying about it now," and Bert walked off, shaking his head and talking with Danny Rugg about girls that couldn't keep a secret.

After all no harm was done, since Mr. Bobbsey wanted the story known, as that might help find Baby May's parents. And besides, as Nan had said, the report would soon get around town on account of the police alarm.

Once the story was known in the school, the Bobbsey twins, even Flossie and Freddie, had to answer many questions as to how Baby May Washington was found on the doorstep.

Nan was quite the heroine of the day, for had not she found the tiny infant crying in the basket?

"Say, Bert, I'll tell you what we can do after school," proposed Charlie Mason that afternoon.

"What?"

"We can scout around and see if we can find that old lady with the green umbrella. We could make her take the baby back."

"Maybe she wouldn't have the green umbrella now, 'cause it isn't raining," said Freddie, who overheard this talk.

"Well, we can look for her, anyhow," went on Charlie. "Will you, Bert?"

"Maybe."

"And maybe there's a reward out for whoever takes this baby back where it lives," suggested Danny Rugg. "Maybe we could get a hundred dollars that way!"

"Most of it would go to Bert, 'cause the baby was found at his house," declared Charlie.

"Well, if we fellows found the old lady, that would count and we'd have part of the reward," declared Tom Carter.

"I don't believe you can find her," said Bert. "I guess she ran away after she left the baby and rang our bell."

This seemed to be the case, for search as the police did, no trace was found of the

strange woman. She had vanished aft
riving in Lakeport and leaving the ba
the Bobbseys' doorstep.

Telephone calls to distant places and
gent reading of the newspapers, failed to
any babies missing or kidnapped. Mr.
sey advertised in the papers of neighb
towns, but when several days had passe
no claim was made for Baby May Was
ton, Mr. Bobbsey and his wife talked the
ter over again.

"There is no trace of who this ch
or to whom she belongs," said the t
father. "I suppose I had better arran
have the police take her to an orphange."

"Well—" began Mrs. Bobbsey slowly
she was interrupted by a chorus of cries
the children.

"Oh, don't send the baby away!"

"Let us keep her!"

"I'll wheel her in my carriage that I
use any more," offered Flossie.

"I like her a little—even if she isn't a
faltered Freddie.

"Please, Mother, let us keep her! Mayn't we, Daddy?" begged Nan.

"She's a cute little thing," murmured Bert. "Hey, Mother! Look! Nan's taking her out of the cradle!" And Nan was doing just this

"Pooh! don't you think I know how to hold a baby?" asked Nan.

"You might if you had a net under you, like the man in the circus, so she wouldn't hit the floor if you dropped her," chuckled Bert.

"Pooh! you think you're smart, don't you?" sneered Nan. This was as near as she and Bert ever came to having a fuss.

"Now, children," chided Mrs. Bobbsey gently, "be polite, please!"

"But what are we going to do with the baby?" asked Mr. Bobbsey. "Nearly a week has gone past now, and we haven't learned any more than we knew the first day. What do you say, Mother?" he asked his wife.

"Of course the baby isn't ours, and we don't know where she belongs," Mrs. Bobbsey said.

"But I have grown to love the little thing, and the children are very fond of her. Suppose we keep Baby May a while longer.

Something may turn up then. I couldn't bear to send her to an orphanage."

"All right," agreed Mr. Bobbsey, with a smile. "Then we'll keep the baby."

"And we'll call her Bobbsey, 'cause she's going to be one of us," added Nan.

"Only she isn't a twin!" added Freddie.

"No, and it's just as well she isn't!" laughed his mother. "I don't know that I'd want to keep *two* little babies, unless they were my own. But I can manage this one very well."

"We'll take care of her," offered Nan, who was quite proud, as she rocked the baby in her arms.

"Could I wheel her in the carriage some time?" asked Flossie.

"I'll see," promised Mrs. Bobbsey.

"She can take my roller skates when she wants them," offered Freddie, and then he wondered why they all laughed. His mother explained:

"Baby May Washington Bobbsey isn't able to walk yet, dear, to say nothing of roller skating. But it was kind of you to offer, Freddie."

"Um!" he murmured. "She'd be better if she was a boy," and he ran out to play.

So the abandoned baby was kept at the Bobbsey house.

"Oh, I think it's terribly romantic to have a strange baby at your house, Nan," said Julia Clark, when she and some other girls were talking about the matter one day at recess. "Just think, she may turn out to be an heiress to a million dollars!"

"And she might turn out to be a gypsy," suggested Grace Lavine.

"She isn't dark enough for a gypsy," said Nan. "And I don't believe she'll ever have a million dollars. Daddy says if she belonged to a wealthy family the papers would be filled with the story about her, and detectives would be searching all over for her."

"Who do you s'pose she is?" asked Nellie.

"Nobody knows," Nan answered, and that was about all that could be said.

There surely was a mystery about Baby May.

As for the little girl herself, she was wonderfully sweet and good-natured. She cried hardly at all, but sat on a blanket on the floor and cooed and gurgled, kicked her rosy feet, fluttered her tiny hands, now and then smiling at the Bobbsey twins who bent over her or played with her.

"When will she be big enough to walk?" asked Freddie.

"Oh, in a few weeks she may begin to toddle," his mother answered. "I don't know just how old she is, but she isn't much over a year. She is growing fast, though."

"She's suttinly de fastest growin' chile whutever I seed!" declared Dinah. "She jes' seem to swell all up when she take her milk. She suah am de mostest darlin' baby! Oh, ain't she cute!" she murmured, bending over the infant.

And "cute" was just the word that described Baby May—Baby May Washington Bobbsey, to give her the name which had been bestowed on her, for the twins now regarded her as one of themselves.

They took care of her after school hours— that is, Flossie and Nan did, for Bert was getting too old to look after babies, he thought.

As for Freddie—well, he hardly could be trusted to do this, as he was such a "splutter-budget," as Dinah called him. She meant he was always hurrying away to have fun, and he might have left Baby May alone to do this.

So to Nan and Flossie fell the happy task of taking care of the baby after school hours. Mrs. Bobbsey would wrap the little one warmly in blankets and put her in Flossie's old carriage. Then Nan or Flossie would wheel her up and down in front of the house, stopping, now and then, to let the other children have a look at Baby May.

As for the little one, she would gaze about, smile and twinkle her blue eyes and say:

"Goo!"

Or perhaps she might, on occasions, say:

"Da!"

And when she said either of these things, whatever they may be called, Flossie or Nan would run into the house or call Mrs. Bobbsey and say, most excitedly:

"Oh, she talked! She talked!"

Once when Bert heard this "talk" he

laughed at his sisters for thinking it meant anything.

"It's just jabbering," he said.

"It isn't!" insisted Nan. "A lot you know! She said 'no' as plain as anything this morning when I offered her some milk, and I'm teaching her to say Nan, and she says 'Na' just as nice!"

"Pooh!" chuckled Bert, as he went out to play ball.

One day, when Mrs. Bobbsey had dressed Baby May and put her out in the baby carriage on the sunny side of the house, Flossie came home from school ahead of Nan.

"Mother, I'm going to wheel Baby May out on the sidewalk!" called Flossie.

Mrs. Bobbsey was busy upstairs with Dinah, and did not hear what Flossie said. If she had heard she might have told Flossie to be very careful.

So, without her mother knowing it, though meaning no wrong, Flossie wheeled Baby May out in the street. The baby was asleep, and Flossie was careful to make no noise as she rolled the carriage to and fro. Then along

came Freddie. He had stopped to play with
some of his boy chums, which was the reason
Flossie had reached home ahead of him.

"I'm going to get my roller skates," Freddie said. "Flossie!" he called, "I can't get
the front gate open. Come and help me!"

"Hush! Don't make so much noise! You'll
wake Baby May!" whispered Flossie, for
Freddie had shouted his request.

"Well, I can't get the gate open!" he repeated.

"I'll help you, but keep quiet!" commanded
Flossie. "Don't wake the baby!"

The front gate stuck sometimes, but Flossie
knew that she and Freddie together could push
it open. So, leaving the baby carriage with
May in it on the sidewalk, the little girl went
to help her brother.

Now, as it happened, the sidewalk ran a little downhill just at this point. And Flossie,
not knowing it, did not put the brake on the
baby-carriage wheels. So, as soon as she
walked away, the carriage, with Baby May in
it, started to roll toward the street at the point
where there was a slanting place to allow Mr.

Bobbsey's automobile to come up over the curbstone.

Down into the street rolled the carriage with the sleeping baby in it, going faster and faster. And up the street, running very fast, came a team of horses hitched to an empty coal wagon. The rumble of the big wagon made Flossie and Freddie, pushing in order to open the gate, look around.

"Oh, look!" shouted Freddie. "It's a runaway! There's nobody in the wagon!"

This was true, and the horses were running faster and faster as they came on up the street toward the Bobbsey house.

"A runaway! A runaway!" cried Freddie, jumping up and down in his excitement.

It was then that Flossie thought of Baby May. She gave one look toward the carriage, and saw it rolling across the street, almost in the path of the dashing horses and the rumbling coal wagon.

"Oh! Oh, dear!" gasped Flossie.

CHAPTER VII

THE SNAP—CRACKER

Freddie Bobbsey dashed away from the front gate, no longer trying to open it. He almost knocked Flossie down, so great was his hurry.

"Oh, what you going to do?" cried the little girl.

"I have to get that carriage and Baby May!" cried Freddie. "If I don't, the horses will run over her!"

"Oh! Oh!" half sobbed Flossie, for she could think of nothing else to do.

The carriage with the baby in it kept on slowly rolling toward the middle of the street. And up the street, running faster and faster, came the excited horses hitched to the empty coal wagon.

"Freddie! Freddie! Don't go out there!"

shrilly cried Flossie, as she saw her little brother about to spring into the street.

"But I have to get the baby!" he insisted.

"All right! Then I'll come with you!" decided Flossie, who had now stopped crying.

She made a dash to join her brother. There was still time to get Baby May and the carriage out of danger if the children hurried. But if they should stumble and fall—

As it happened, Bert Bobbsey came whistling around the corner just at that moment. Bert was thinking of going fishing, and he always whistled at such times. When Flossie and Freddie caught sight of their brother, they stopped running, feeling sure he could and would save Baby May.

Bert's whistle died away when he caught sight of the dashing, runaway horses and saw them swaying the empty wagon from side to side. Several men and boys were racing after the runaways, shouting, as if that would stop them. Other men and boys dashed out in front, waving their hats and arms, which only frightened the horses the more.

Then Bert saw the baby carriage, now almost in the middle of the street and directly in the path of the runaways.

"Crickity grasshoppers!" shouted Bert. "It's Baby May! I've got to save her!"

Wisely, he did not try to stop the runaways. This was more than a boy of Bert's age could have done. Instead, he gave his whole attention to getting the carriage out of the way. This was easy enough to do if, as Bert said afterward, you had "nerve" enough. It meant dashing across the street, pushing the carriage ahead of him, right across the path of the runaways.

But Bert did just that! He ran as fast as he could—faster than he had ever run when playing ball—and reached the carriage just in time. He could hear Baby May cooing and gurgling to herself amid the blankets. She never knew what danger she was in. She liked the easy, rolling motion of the baby carriage.

"Look out there, little boy!" cried a man, who was racing after the runaways.

"I must get our baby!" shouted Bert.

The next moment he had hold of the handle

of the carriage.   Never slacking his fast run, he pushed it out of danger, to the other side of the street.   There was not much time to spare, either, for before Bert reached the opposite gutter the runaway team dashed past his heels.   But he was safe and so was Baby May.

"Hey, boy, that was a brave thing to do!" cried one of the several men who were trying to stop the runaways.

"Um!" was all Bert could answer, for he was out of breath.

Then, as the coal wagon team dashed on up the street, Bert wheeled the carriage back to where Flossie and Freddie waited.

"Who had Baby May out?" Bert wanted to know.

"I did," answered Flossie.   "Mother said I could, and—"

"Well, what do you want to take her out in the street for when runaways come along?" asked Bert, who seemed a bit angry.

"I didn't take the baby carriage out in the street!" whimpered Flossie, half crying.   "It—

now—it rolled there when I was trying to help Freddie open the gate."

"And I was going out to get her," added Freddie.

"Well, you two want to be careful," said Bert, more kindly, as he noticed how frightened the younger twins were. "Come on now, we'll go back to the house."

"I want to see if they caught the runaways," insisted Freddie.

Bert looked up the street and saw a man leading the team back. The horses were quiet enough now. They had become tired, had slowed down, and had easily been stopped.

"They're all right—no damage done," said Bert. "But you two have got to be more careful with Baby May. She might have been run over."

"I'll be more careful after this," promised Flossie.

"So will I," added Freddie, though it really was not his fault.

Mrs. Bobbsey was told what had happened—or rather, what had so nearly happened—and she decided that Flossie was too young to take Baby May out unless some older person was at hand to watch for danger.

Baby May cooed and smiled when she was lifted out of the baby carriage to be fed, and she made funny faces at Freddie and clutched at his nose with her soft little hand, causing Freddie to squirm, partly in delight and partly because she tickled him.

The days passed with no word as to who Baby May was. All that Mr. Bobbsey and the police did to find the parents of the little baby went for nothing.

"I guess, Mother," said Mr. Bobbsey to his wife, "we'll have to keep this baby a long time."

"I don't care how long we keep her," was the answer. "I've grown to love her!"

Bert and Nan, as well as Flossie and Freddie, also loved Baby May, and they hoped nothing would ever take her from them. Though of course they agreed with their father that if the child's mother and father could be found, they must have Baby May.

"Shall we take her with us when we go on

our vacation, after school stops?" asked Bert of his mother, one morning.

"Perhaps," she answered. "But you'd better hurry now, or you may be late for school."

But, to tell the truth, Bert did not hurry very much. The days were getting more like summer all the while—warm and filled with sunshine—and perhaps this is the reason why Bert lingered on the way to school. But so did other boys and girls.

And perhaps this is the reason why Bert, in class that day, did not pay much attention to what was going on. It was the time for geography study, and the boys and girls had on their desks in front of them the large books, for they were learning to pick out places on the map of Africa.

Now the big geographies were large enough to hide behind, and perhaps you have done what many children have done at times—that is, you have read or written notes in the shadow of the covers of the big books held up in front of you.

Bert did not care about writing any notes,

and he had none written by any other boy to read.   But he had in his pocket a piece of tough, brown paper, and, almost before he knew it, Bert was folding this paper into what he called a "snap-cracker."

As you boys and girls must know how to make them I will not take the time to tell you how it is done.   But by folding his paper in a certain way, Bert at length had it in the shape of a triangle, with an inner fold that, when he brought the hand holding the paper down quickly and stopped it suddenly, would snap out with a pop like that of a bursting paper bag.

Bert made this snap-cracker and then he looked across the aisle.   Danny Rugg sat there, and Danny was a mischievous fellow.

"I dare you to crack that!" whispered Danny to Bert.

"I will after school!" Bert whispered back. It was safe to whisper behind the big geographies.

"No, I mean crack it now!" went on Danny. "I double-dare you!"

Bert did not like to take a dare.   Much less

did he like to be "double-dared." He peered over the top of his big book. The teacher was busy at some papers on her desk.

Slowly Bert raised the paper snapper as high as he dared. Then, swinging his arm out into the aisle, where there was plenty of room, he brought his hand down smartly, checking it half way.

Bang! went the snap-cracker, with a noise like a pistol shot.

"Oh!" gasped a number of the pupils.

Some of them laughed out loud.

The teacher looked up quickly from her desk.

"Who did that?" she asked quietly.

There was no answer for a moment.

"I want the boy or girl who did that to come up here to my desk," went on the teacher.

The room was very still and quiet.

CHAPTER VIII

THE OLD WOMAN AGAIN

SEVERAL boys and girls seated near Bert had seen him snap the paper cracker. Of course they would never "tell on him," but they gave him sidelong glances to see if he would accept the "invitation" of the teacher.

"I am waiting," went on Miss Riker, in a quiet voice. "I want the boy—I don't think it was one of the girls—I want that boy to come up to my desk."

The room again became very still and quiet.

And then, slowly, like the little man he was, Bert arose in his seat. He was rather pale, for he realized that he had done a wrong thing. But he was not going to sneak out of it.

"I snapped the cracker, Miss Riker," he said slowly.

"Oh, Bert! I'm so sorry!" was the teacher's answer. "Come up here and sit in the front seat. The others go on studying."

That was Miss Riker's way. She never punished a pupil at once when rules were broken. She wanted to think over it quietly and have the pupil think of it, so she always asked the boy or girl who had been disobedient to come to the front seat.

Bert knew what this meant. He would be kept in after school, perhaps made to write "disorderly" five hundred times or do some other "punish lesson." And he was trying so hard for a perfect mark this last month of school! Too bad!

Well, it was his own fault—he knew that. Slowly he made his way to the front seat, the eyes of every other boy and girl in the room looking at him. Miss Riker did not look at him. That would come later.

"Five minutes more of study and then I'll hear the geography class," Miss Riker announced, and this set the laggard ones feverishly to studying, some murmuring over and over again the location of the Cape of Good Hope, which was the easiest thing to remember about Africa.

Bert was not allowed to recite with the

others.   He was kept in the front seat and began to feel very uncomfortable.   He wished Miss Riker would tell him how she was going to punish him, and have it over with.

But when the time came to dismiss the pupils for the day, the teacher said:

"You may all go now except Bert Bobbsey."

This was to be expected.

Slowly Nan, with a sad look on her face for her brother's plight, marched out of the room with the others.   Miss Riker busied herself with some papers at her desk.   Bert sat in the front seat.   Then the teacher, looking up, saw Danny Rugg in his seat.   He had remained after the others.

"Why, Danny!" exclaimed Miss Riker in surprise, "I didn't tell you to stay in.   You didn't snap a paper cracker, did you?"

"No'm," murmured Danny rather bashfully. "But I—I doubled-dared Bert to snap his, and that's why he did it.   I—now—I wanted to tell you."

"Oh!" was all Miss Riker said, but there was a strange look on her face.

"Yes'm," murmured Danny, though, really, he did not know why he said it.

Again the room became very quiet, only the clock ticked loudly—oh, so loudly!

Then, with a smile, Miss Riker said:

"Well, Bert, I think you needn't stay in any longer. I was going to give you a punish lesson, but as long as Danny has been brave enough to remain and confess his part of it— though really you shouldn't do a thing just because you are dared to do it—I think, after all, that I will let you both go home. You won't crack any more snappers—or snap any more crackers—in school hours, will you, Bert?"

"No'm! Never any more!" he said very earnestly.

"And you won't dare him again, Danny?"

"No'm! I never will—in school!"

"Then you both may go."

"Thank you," mumbled the boys, as they found their caps and departed. Miss Riker smiled. She knew this had been the best "punish lesson" she could have set.

"Say, wasn't she nice!" exclaimed Danny, when he and Bert were outside.

"Crickity grasshoppers, she sure was!" declared Bert. "I didn't exactly mean to snap that cracker, anyhow."

"I didn't think you'd do it, even after I doubled-dared you," remarked Danny.

"I was just going to make believe, but when my arm got going I couldn't seem to stop it," explained Bert. "Say, did it cra k loud?"

"Loud? It was like a gun!" And both boys laughed.

Of course Bert had to tell his mother, for she asked why he was late coming from school. She warned him to be more careful and to pay better attention to his lessons, but she did not scold. She thought Miss Riker knew how to manage her pupils.

The next day was Friday, and when the hour for geography study came in Miss Riker's room she rather surprised the pupils by saying:

"You need not take out your geographies this time." Then, as she saw surprised looks cast at Bert she added: "It isn't because of

what happened yesterday. Bert isn't going
to crack any more snappers. But I'm going
to teach you geography in a new way. We
are all going out to Pine Hill and from there we
can look down on Lake Metoka. We shall see
little bays, capes, peninsulas, islands, and many
other formations that you have been studying
about in the geography class. Now we are
really going to see them as they are in nature."

You can imagine what delightful excitement there was then! To study outside the
classroom! What a change! Miss Riker led
forth the boys and girls, and, as they left the
school yard, marching two by two as they did
at fire drill, the teacher further surprised her
pupils by saying:

"You may talk all you wish, but I'd rather
you would talk about something connected
with geography. If any of you see a brook
that looks like a little river, tell the rest
of us."

More wonders! To be allowed to go out of
the classroom in school hours and then to talk!
The children could hardly believe it. Miss

Riker heard Nan Bobbsey and Nellie P
timidly whispering.

"You may talk out loud," she said, smil

Was it possible? It was, as the boys
girls soon found out. And then, how
talked!

"I see a brook!" cried Nan, presently.

"Yes, and I see a pond that might almos
a lake," added one of the other girls.

"Yes, and there's an island in the lake,"
in Bert, quickly, and he pointed to a small
of dirt in the center of the pond. This ren
made everybody laugh.

"I see a cliff," said another boy, and poi
to the edge of a steep hill.

From Pine Hill they could look down or
lake and could see many natural format
that, in miniature, resembled the larger
told about in the geography. Miss Riker
the boys and girls name the different fo
tions of land and water.

"It was the nicest lesson we ever had!"
Nan Bobbsey, at home that night.

"Dandy!" declared Bert. "I wish
take us fishing some time!"

"Maybe she will!" chuckled Mr. Bobbsey.

"Hush! Not so loud!" cautioned Mrs. Bobbsey, coming from a bedroom. "I've just gotten Baby May to sleep!"

The next day was Saturday, and of course there was no school.

"Though if it was all like the geography lesson yesterday I wouldn't mind going to school on Saturdays," said Bert, as he looked for his cap to go out to play.

"Neither would I," agreed Nan. "Mother, may I take Baby May out in the baby carriage?" she asked.

"In a little while you and Flossie may wheel her," said Mrs. Bobbsey. "I don't like Flossie to take her alone, as she's been teasing to do."

"Well, I'm going over and play ball with the other boys," announced Bert.

Just then the telephone rang.

"It's your father," announced Mrs. Bobbsey, after listening a moment. "He says," she went on, "that he has to go to Menton on some business in the auto, and he wants to know if you two would like to ride with him," and she looked at Bert and Nan. Flossie and Freddie were out in the yard playing.

"Oh, would we!" cried Nan, clasping her hands in joyful anticipation. "When is he coming?"

"I'd rather ride with dad than play ball," declared Bert.

"You're to go down to the lumberyard and he'll wait for you there," said Mrs. Bobbsey. "Don't say anything about it to Flossie or Freddie, else they'll tease to go, and I can't let them."

So Bert and Nan departed quietly by the side gate and were soon hurrying to their father's office on the lumber dock that extended out a long way into Lake Metoka.

"What to you suppose daddy's going over to Menton for?" asked Nan.

"Oh, he buys lumber there," replied Bert, who had been to this neighboring city once or twice before with his father. "I guess that's what he's going to do this time."

And this, the children learned when they reached the office, was exactly Mr. Bobbsey's errand to Menton. This city was about fifteen miles from Lakeport.

"Well, children, I hope I didn't take you away from your studies or your home work," said Mr. Bobbsey, with a smile, as Nan and Bert walked up to where he waited in the car.

"Oh, Daddy! As if we'd study on *Saturday!*" cried Nan.

"Not me!" declared Bert.

"Then we'll declare a holiday!" laughed their father. "All aboard!"

It was a pleasant day, the roads were good, and they had a delightful trip to Menton. Bert and Nan were treated to ice-cream soda in a drug store while their father did what business he had to look after. Then they started back.

As they drove past the Menton railroad station Nan suddenly caught hold of her father's arm and exclaimed:

"Look! There she is again!"

"Who?" asked Mr. Bobbsey.

"That old lady—the one with the faded shawl and the green umbrella—the old woman who left Baby May on our doorstep!" gasped Nan excitedly.

"Where is she?" her father cried.

"Look! She's just getting on the train," said Nan, for a train was about to leave the station.

"Oh, I see her!" cried Bert. "It's the same old woman!"

"I must stop her! I must speak to her!" cried Mr. Bobbsey. "It's lucky you saw her! I say there! Hi, madam! I want to talk to you! Wait a minute!" he called loudly, as he drove the automobile as close to the track as he dared go.

CHAPTER IX

IN PURSUIT

BEFORE Mr. Bobbsey could bring his automobile to a stop, and almost as soon as the old woman in the faded shawl was on the platform of one of the cars, the engine tooted twice and the train began to move.

"Oh, she's going to get away!" exclaimed Bert.

"Stop the train!" cried Nan. "Somebody stop the train!"

Mr. Bobbsey brought his automobile to a standstill by a sudden pull on the emergency brake. Then he jumped out and ran swiftly across the depot platform toward the moving train.

"Wait a minute! Stop! I want to speak to you! I want that old lady in the faded shawl!" he cried, for now the strange old woman was out of sight, inside one of the cars.

89

"Look out, sir! Don't try to get on that moving train!" cried one of the railroad men, stepping in front of Mr. Bobbsey. "It's dangerous!"

"I don't want to get on the train! I want to get a passenger off the train—the little old lady in the faded shawl," explained Mr. Bobbsey.

"Sorry, sir, but it's too late. The train's going too fast and I can't stop it," the railroad man said.

And as Nan and Bert, seated in the automobile, watched, they saw the train gathering speed. It was carrying farther and farther away from them the strange woman—the woman who could solve the mystery of Baby May.

"Well, I guess I'm too late," sighed Mr. Bobbsey, in disappointed tones as he watched the train disappear from sight around a curve. "If I had only been a minute or two sooner! But there's no use worrying, I suppose," he added.

"Is there any trouble?" asked the railroad man. "Was that lady your wife?"

"Oh, no," answered Mr. Bobbsey, with a smile. "I just wanted to get some information from her. Where does that train go?" he asked. "And where does it stop first?"

"It goes to Brockton," the railroad man replied. "And the first stop is Miles Junction. Were you thinking of trying to catch up to it in your auto?"

"Oh, no. But I think I will send a telegram to the conductor and ask him about the old woman. He'll surely be able to pick her out from the other passengers. I want to get her name and address so I can talk to her. There is something of great importance I want to ask her."

"It would be a good idea to telegraph on ahead to the conductor," said the railroad man. "The train dispatcher will do the telegraphing for you. The conductor's name is Jerry Simpson. The old woman didn't rob you, or anything like that, did she?"

"Oh, no!" laughed Mr. Bobbsey. "Nothing like that!" But he did not tell why he wanted to find out who she was. There was no need of mentioning Baby May.

"What are you going to do, Daddy?" asked
Bert, as his father returned to the automobile,
the engine of which was still running.

Mr. Bobbsey told the children his plans, add-
ing:

"While I am waiting for the train conductor
to telegraph back to me, I'll make some inquiries around here to see if I can find out
anything about the old woman."

"And shall we have dinner when we get
back home?" asked Nan.

"Dinner! Good gracious! Here it is nearly
noon!" exclaimed Mr. Bobbsey, looking at his
watch. "Well, we can get a lunch here while
waiting for an answer to my telegram. And I
guess I'd better telephone your mother to let
her know we shall be delayed. This is the first
chance I've had to get on the trail of the
strange old woman, and I don't want to miss
it."

Mr. Bobbsey sent a telegram to Miles Junction for Jerry Simpson, conductor of the train,
asking him to wire back the name and address
of the old woman in the faded shawl. She
did not have the green umbrella with her this

time, and of course the big basket, in which Baby May had been left, was at the Bobbsey home.

In his telegram Mr. Bobbsey asked the conductor to send word back in care of the train dispatcher at Menton. This having been done, the twins' father began to make inquiries of railroad men and others about the strange woman.

None of them knew her, and few of them had noticed her coming to the station to take the train. So his questions did not bring him much information.

"We must wait for an answer to the telegram," said Mr. Bobbsey.

"And can we eat now?" asked Bert. "I'm mighty hungry."

"I'm hungry, too," added Nan.

"You certainly shall eat!" laughed their father, and he took them to a restaurant.

They had to wait nearly an hour for the answer to come back from the conductor, as the Miles Junction stop of the train was many miles away. But finally, as the three sat in the station, waiting, the train dispatcher came out of his little office, where a hundred clocks seemed ticking. In his hand he held a paper.

"Are you Mr. Bobbsey?" he asked.

"Yes," replied the twins' father.

"Oh, yes, I remember you. You sent a message to Mr. Simpson on train thirty-two. Well, here's his answer."

"Thank you," said Mr. Bobbsey. "Any charge?"

"No charge."

The dispatcher went back to his clicking instruments. Mr. Bobbsey read the message to himself.

"What does it say, Daddy?" Bert ventured to ask.

"Will she come back and tell us about the baby?" Nan wanted to know. "Will she take Baby May away from us?"

"This isn't a message from the strange woman—it's from the train conductor," answered Mr. Bobbsey. "It says that the old woman in the faded shawl got off at Hankertown. Um! I thought the train didn't stop this side of Miles Junction, but it must have done so."

"Where's Hankertown?" asked Bert.

"About fifteen miles from here," his father said. "Wait until I ask the dispatcher about this."

The dispatcher, who was also the ticket seller explained that sometimes the train stopped at way stations, before reaching Miles Junction, in case there were passengers to get off or on.

"And that's what must have happened in this case," the dispatcher gave as his opinion. "The party you inquired about must have had a ticket to Hankertown, and that's why she got off there. Is there anything more I can do for you?"

"Thank you—no," answered Mr. Bobbsey. "Come, children," he called to Bert and Nan.

"Where are you going?" they asked him.

"I'm going to keep on after the little old lady. I must find her! We can go to Hankertown by auto. It's only fifteen miles."

"It isn't as far as that if you go by the back road," the train dispatcher told them. "It's fifteen miles by railroad, about the same by the main highway, but much less by the back road."

"Is it a good road?" questioned Mr. Bobbsey.

"Fair," answered the dispatcher. "You'll make time if you take the back road."

"That's what I'll do, then," said Mr. Bobbsey.

He had already telephoned to his wife, telling her that they had caught sight of the strange woman who had deserted the baby.

"I'm going to make her tell the secret!" said Mr. Bobbsey.

"What about Nan and Bert?" asked Mrs. Bobbsey, over the wire.

"I'll keep them with me," their father replied. "They'll be all right—don't worry. Are Flossie and Freddie all right?"

"Yes; only Freddie fell in a mud puddle and pulled Flossie in after him! They're sights, but that's nothing new!"

"Is the baby all right?"

"Oh, yes, she's a little darling. I almost hope we never have to give her up—but of course we must do what is right."

So it was that Mr. Bobbsey with Bert and Nan started for Hankertown in the automobile, trying to arrive as soon as possible after the train had left the strange, old woman there. But, as the train had gone on to Miles Junction before the conductor received the telegram, the old woman might have disappeared again.

"Do you think she lives in Hankertown?" asked Nan, as the automobile dashed along the country road.

"She may," answered Mr. Bobbsey. "Even if she doesn't, some one there will be sure to know her and we can find out about her from them. At least I hope so."

"I do, too," murmured Nan. "But I love Baby May!"

"She's awfully cute!" exclaimed Bert. "You ought to see her grab hold of my nose! She holds on so tight!" And he laughed at the remembrance.

Mr. Bobbsey was driving the car along at as fast a pace as was safe, and they were about half way to Hankertown when Bert noticed little jets of vapor coming from the radiator.

"Look, Dad!" he exclaimed. "She's steaming!"

"Whew!" whistled Mr. Bobbsey. "I'm out of water! Must stop and get some right away! It won't do to overheat the engine!"

He stopped the car, and at once a loud hissing was heard while from beneath the car a big cloud of steam poured out.

"Oh! are we on fire?" screamed Nan.

CHAPTER X

"Don't be silly, Nan!" exclaimed Bert, as he held his sister back. She seemed about to leap from the car, which Mr. Bobbsey had already left.

"What do you mean—silly?" demanded Nan, a bit angrily.

"Because the car isn't on fire—is it, Daddy?" he appealed to his father.

"Of course not!" replied Mr. Bobbsey. "It was stupid of me, but I forgot to put water in the radiator. What little there was in there has become so hot that it has boiled and turned into steam. Now the steam is simply escaping through the overflow pipe, which comes out beneath the front axle. Here, Nan, come and look at it, and you'll know what it is the next time."

"Oh," murmured Bert's sister, feeling the

least little bit ashamed of herself because she had been frightened. Then she got out, Bert helping her politely, and looked to where the steam in a white cloud was hissing its way out of a small pipe.

"No danger at all, if you don't run too long after your water begins to boil," explained Mr. Bobbsey. "But I've got to get a fresh supply. I wonder if there's a roadside spring anywhere around here?"

"I'll look," offered Bert.

"So'll I," chimed in Nan.

"Well, then," agreed their father, "one of you go a little way up the road and the other a little way down the road. Don't go too far, if you don't find water. I'll stay here by the car and take the cap off the radiator. That will let the steam out more quickly."

The two Bobbsey twins separated, going in different directions along the lonely country road.

"Doesn't seem to be much chance of getting water here," thought Bert, as he trudged along. "It's as dry as a desert."

This was true. There had been no rain for

some time—not more than little showers since
the big storm in which Baby May came—and
the grass and weeds along the road were dry
and dusty.

Nan, too, looked in vain for a spring or a
brook where her father could scoop up water
in the folding canvas pail he carried under the
seat of the automobile.

"I wonder what we'll do if daddy can't get
water," Nan was thinking, when she rounded
a turn in the road and saw, in the midst of a
clump of apple trees, a small house almost like
a log cabin save that it was built of boards instead of logs.

"Oh, I guess some one must live there,"
thought Nan. "And if they do they must have
a well of water. I'll go and ask, to make sure,
before I go back and tell daddy."

She made her way toward the weather-
beaten, paintless hut, going slowly for fear
some savage dog might rush out at her. But
none came, and she opened the gate. The gate
swung shut after her. It was pulled by a
piece of iron fastened to a bit of clothesline
for a weight.

"Who's comin' in my yard?" a shrill voice demanded—the voice of an old woman, Nan decided, for she could see no one. For a moment, she thought it might be the woman in the faded shawl, the woman who had deserted the baby. Was it possible that little May had come from here?

"Who's comin' in my yard?" the voice went on. Nan felt that she must answer.

"If you please, could we get some water—for the auto?" faltered Nan. "It's boiling over—I mean the auto is—and it needs cool water, and—"

She stopped suddenly as an old woman came around the path that twined itself around the house. One look showed Nan that it was not the little old woman of the faded shawl. This was quite a different person, in fact.

"What is it you want?" demanded the old woman sharply.

"Some water, if you please, for my father's auto. It's just down the road a little way," replied Nan.

"Oh, water! I s'pose ye heard of my spring, ain't ye?" said the woman, in a rasping voice.

"Your spring? No, I didn't know you had a spring," answered Nan. "But I thought maybe you might have a well, and—"

"I ain't got a well; but I've a fine deep spring, an' the water's as cold as ice. But, say, look here! Did you ever throw stones at my frog?" The old woman asked this question sharply.

"Your frog! No!" gasped Nan, wondering whether or not she might have to do with a crazy person. "I never saw your frog," she added.

"Oh, all right then," said the woman, more gently. "Girls ain't so bad as boys. It's the pesky boys that's allers throwin' stones at my frog. He's the biggest bullfrog you ever saw. Him an' me's friends, an' I never let anybody get a drink from my spring that has throwed stones at my frog. Seein' as how you ain't, you can have all the water you want. Come, I'll show you where the spring is."

She started to lead the way down a weed-tangled path at the side of the house, but Nan drew back. She did not exactly like this old woman with that queer story about a giant frog.

"I'll—I'll go call my father," said Nan. "He'll get the water in a pail, thank you. I'll call my father," and she turned away.

"Your father never throwed stones at my frog, did he?" demanded the old woman sharply. Nan decided she was so queer that she must be a hermit—living all alone in the half-tumbled-down hut.

"Of course not!" exclaimed Nan. "Daddy wouldn't throw stones at any animal."

"Wa-all, mebby he did when he was a boy. But I'll let him get some water from my spring," said the old woman.

Before Nan could reach the swinging gate she heard her father calling, and Bert, too, added his voice, saying:

"Nan! Nan! Did you find any water?"

"Yes, there's a spring here," Nan replied, "But—"

She was going to add something about the frog, but she did not have time, for her father and Bert at that moment opened the gate. They caught sight of the old woman.

For a moment, Bert said later, he thought she was the one for whom they were searching. But he had no time to say anything for no sooner had the old woman caught sight of Bert, than she exclaimed:

"Oh, ho! There's a boy! A pesky boy! Did you ever throw stones at my frog in the spring? If ye did——"

"No, I never did!" declared Bert.

"Are ye sure?"

"Sure!" he repeated, wondering what it all meant.

"What's this about a frog in the spring?" asked Mr. Bobbsey, smiling, for he saw that he had to do with a queer person.

"It's my frog, Ebenezer," explained the old woman. "The biggest bullfrog that ever lived. I'll show him to you and let you get water from my spring if you never throwed stones at him."

"I'm sure we never did, for I have never been on this road before," answered Mr. Bobbsey.

The old woman looked at him sharply, then

at Bert; and, as if satisfied that they were telling the truth, she said:

"Wa-all, all right. Come on and bring your
blickie."

"My blickie?" exclaimed Mr. Bobbsey.
"What's that?"

"Your pail—your bucket—whatever you
call it. I calls 'em blickies. That's what I
calls 'em—blickies," said the old woman. "It's
Dutch—Pennsylvania Dutch," she explained.
"I'm Pennsylvania Dutch."

"Oh," murmured Mr. Bobbsey, making a
side motion to Nan and Bert to tell them not
to laugh.

The old woman shuffled along, leading the
way down the weed- and vine-obstructed path
until she pointed to a stone-lined hole in the
ground, near a small shed.

"There's the spring," she said. "Help yourself. Fill your blickie," and she motioned to
the canvas pail in Mr. Bobbsey's hand. "But
it's the queerest blickie I ever see. And don't
you bother my frog!" she warned.

Mr. Bobbsey and the children hardly knew
whether or not to believe that there was a frog.

But when Mr. Bobbsey leaned over the edge of the deep, clear spring, to fill the canvas pail, he saw, sitting on the bottom, in the clean, white sand, the largest frog he had ever beheld.

"Look, children!" he said. "It is a giant frog!"

And so it was—an immense green bullfrog, that looked at them with its bulging, fishy eyes from the bottom of the pool. Perhaps the water magnified the frog, making it appear larger than it really was, but it certainly seemed immense.

"That's my pet frog," mumbled the old woman. "I don't let no boys stone him if I can help it, but sometimes I can't help it. They peg rocks at him when he sits on the edge of the spring. An' if I ketch them boys—wa-all, if they do it once they never can drink from my spring again."

"What boys are they?" asked Mr. Bobbsey, as he filled his canvas pail, the frog not seeming to be disturbed.

"Oh, pesky boys—boys what go up in the hills to take their cows to pasture or drive 'em home. Pesky boys," answered the old woman.

"Well, I never stoned any frogs," said Bert.

"Then you must be one of the few good boys," said the old woman, and she gave a half-smile, for the first time in many days it seemed.

"Thank you for the water," said Mr. Bobbsey, as he started off with the dripping pail.

"Ef the children want any there's a dipper in the spring house," said the old woman.

"I'd like a drink," said Bert.

"Oh," murmured Nan. "Would you take a drink from the spring where that big frog is?"

"Sure!" answered her brother. "A frog is as clean as a fish, and all the water we drink has fishes in it."

"Does it, Daddy?" asked Nan.

"Of course," laughed Mr. Bobbsey. "The frog doesn't hurt the water any."

"Then I'll take a drink," decided Nan. And they all drank, finding the water cool—almost ice-cold, in fact—and delicious.

"Come ag'in any time ye like as long as ye

don't stone my frog," invited the old woman.

"Thank you," said Mr. Bobbsey.

The automobile was much cooler by the time they went back to it, and pouring the cold spring water into the radiator enabled them to go on without further delay. Bert told Nan that, when he could find no water on his part of the road, he went back to the car and Mr. Bobbsey, and then the two of them went in search of Nan, who had walked a bit farther than her brother.

"She was a queer old character," said Mr. Bobbsey, as he drove the machine along toward Hankertown. "Lives all alone, I guess, except for her giant frog."

Later he learned that the woman, while considered partly crazy, was a good and harmless old soul with a horror of boys who might stone her frog—as, alas, many of the lads did.

Without further mishap Hankertown was reached, and Mr. Bobbsey decided to begin his inquiries at the railroad station, since it was there the little old lady in the faded shawl had left the train.

The station at Hankertown was a small

one—there did not seem to be much business
done there—and Mr. Bobbsey decided that the
agent would probably remember having seen
the old lady. He might even know her name
and where she lived.

But when the twins' father had told the
agent what was wanted, asking if he knew the
strange woman, the agent said:

"No, I can't say I know her. But I do
remember seeing her get off the train. She
had a shawl, just as you describe."

"Which way did she go?" asked Mr. Bobbsey. "Does she live in the village?"

"I can't say, I'm sure. I don't know where
she lives. But she went up the wood road
after she left the train."

"Which is the wood road?" Mr. Bobbsey
wanted to know. "It is very important that
I find this old woman, or I should not trouble
you with so many questions," he said.

"Oh, that's all right," answered the station
agent, good-naturedly. "I'm used to answering questions. That's why I'm here. The
wood road is that one crossing the track and

going up though the woods," he explained, pointing.

Then Mr. Bobbsey and the children noticed it—a narrow, winding road, half hidden amid the trees.

"Where does it lead to?" asked Mr. Bobbsey.

"Well, if you keep on it long enough, and don't turn off on any of the side trails, it will take you to Coopertown."

"Hum—yes. I know that place. They make a lot of barrels there," said Mr. Bobbsey.

"But it's thirty miles to Coopertown, and there are a lot of little villages in between," said the agent. "But be sure to keep to the main road."

"I will," replied Mr. Bobbsey. "Thank you."

He was about to start on again in the automobile with the children, hoping to overtake the strange woman, when Bert saw a lunch wagon not far from the station.

"Daddy, I'm hungry!" he cried.

"So'm I," added Nan.

"Yes? Well, I could eat a sandwich my-

self," Mr. Bobbsey said. "I'll get some at the
wagon, and some bottles of soda, and we'll eat
as we go along. I don't want to delay, for
that old woman may disappear again."

He bought some things at the lunch wagon,
and started once more, driving through the
woods. The road was a fair one, of dirt, but
so narrow that the branches of the trees on
either side brushed the children as they passed.

"I wouldn't like to meet a big truck now,"
said Mr. Bobbsey, as they reached a very narrow place and squeezed through. "There is
no room to pass."

But they met no other cars, and heard none.
It was very still and quiet in the road, save
for the chugging of their own motor and the
occasional notes of birds.

"Daddy, it's getting late, isn't it?" asked
Nan, when they had gone several miles, with
never a sign of the old woman. They had
not even passed a house at which they might
inquire.

"My gracious, it is late—nearly six
o'clock!" exclaimed Mr. Bobbsey, looking at
his watch. "We've been traveling the best

part of the day. Whew! I don't know whether we'd better go on or not. It doesn't look very promising ahead," he added, as he slowed down the car. "We're getting deeper into the woods all the while."

"Do you think the old woman came along here?" asked Bert.

"It's hard to say, Son," answered his father. "I'll keep on a bit farther, and then, if we don't catch up to her, I'll turn back."

They went on for another mile, and then, finding a good place to turn, Mr. Bobbsey did so.

"Guess we'll have to give it up," he said. "That agent spoke of several towns or villages between Hankertown and Coopertown, but we haven't seen a single house. Yes, I'll turn back."

It was getting dusk now, and Mr. Bobbsey turned on the lights. He peered from side to side of the road, and tooted his horn at curves. Suddenly Nan exclaimed:

"Daddy, we didn't pass that big rock before. Look!"

"That's right," her father admitted, as they

swung around a boulder as large as a small house. "Whew, this is bad! I was afraid of this!"

"What's the matter?" asked Bert.

"I'm afraid we took the wrong road," his father replied.

"Are we lost—in the woods?" faltered Nan.

"It begins to look that way," her father answered. "Yes, it surely begins to look as though we were lost!"

CHAPTER XI

ADVENTURES OF THE NIGHT

MR. BOBBSEY brought the automobile to a
stop not far from the great rock which Nan
had first caught sight of. She did not remember to have passed it earlier in the trip, and
this fact caused her to think they had come
back by another road. And she was right.

"What are you going to do, Daddy?" asked
Bert, as he saw his father getting out of the
car.

"I'm going to look around a bit," was the
answer. "There may be a sign near this rock,
telling us where we are. I don't very often
get lost, but I suppose I was thinking so much
of the strange woman we are after that I
didn't pay proper heed to the road."

"S'posing there isn't any sign?" asked Nan.

"Well, we'll wait and see whether there is
or not before we look for trouble," laughed

Mr. Bobbsey. His laugh made Nan and Bert feel better.

There was still a little, lingering light where the trees did not quite meet in an arch overhead in the road, and by this faint glow Mr. Bobbsey looked around the rock for some sign that would tell him which direction to take to get to the nearest town.

But he saw no sign. The big rock jutted out from the side of a hill, around which the wood road turned, but there was no signboard or post—nothing to tell travelers where they were.

"Um," said Mr. Bobbsey to himself, as he came back to the automobile where Nan and Bert waited. "This isn't very pleasant."

"What are you going to do?" asked Bert, as he watched his father turning on the ignition to get ready to start the car.

"I'm going to drive on a little way and see if we don't get somewhere, or reach a cross road that will take us to a town," said Mr. Bobbsey. "If I don't find one within a mile or two I'll turn and go the other way—back from here," and he pointed over the road they had just traveled.

"I hope you find a road," murmured Nan. "I don't want to stay in these woods all night."

"Crickity grasshoppers! I think it would be fun," laughed Bert. "Look, we have plenty of sandwiches left!"

He showed several in a bag.

"Perhaps it's a good thing we have them," said his father. "There is no restaurant around here, I'm sure."

"We have three bottles of soda water left, too," went on Bert. He had bought more than was really needed for lunch.

Mr. Bobbsey drove the car carefully along the road. It was rapidly growing darker, and the lights of the automobile made two gleaming paths through the gloom.

"There doesn't seem to be anything down this way," said the twins' father, after going about two miles. "Now we'll try it in the other direction from the big rock."

But that plan, likewise, amounted to nothing. Not a cross road did they see which they might take and so get to some town or village. And Mr. Bobbsey did not want to go too far back lest he get in a worse place than near the great stone.

"Well, we seem to be in the midst of a deserted wilderness," he said, as once more he drove the car back to the big stone. "I guess we'd better stay here."

"Oh! All night?" faltered Nan.

"Well, it won't be light until morning," her father said, with a laugh. "And we'd only get more confused and lost, if that's possible, traveling in the darkness. Cheer up, little girl, it won't be so bad!"

"I think it will be sport!" declared Bert. "We can sleep in the car, and we've got something to eat. Can I make a campfire, Daddy?"

"No, I hardly think we will need that, and you might set fire to the woods—they are very dry. We have nothing to cook, and the car lamps will give us light enough."

"No, we haven't anything to cook—only some sandwiches to eat," murmured Bert. "But it's lucky we have them!" he added.

"Yes, I think it is," his father said.

Mr. Bobbsey backed the car under an overhanging ledge of the great rock off the road, so that, if necessary, other cars could pass them in the night.

"But I hardly think other cars will come along," said the children's father. "I guess ours is the only auto within fifteen miles."

"How shall we ever get home?" asked Nan.

"Oh, I can see to find my way out well enough when morning comes," said her father. "It's just that I don't want to drive on a strange road after dark, and in the forest. Now then, let's get ready to camp out for the night."

"What will mother think when we don't come home?" asked Nan.

"She may worry a little," Mr. Bobbsey replied. "But she will know you children are all right as long as you are with me. She'll guess what has happened—that we have either had a breakdown or are lost. Your mother won't worry too much, I think."

Mr. Bobbsey's automobile was a large touring car, and there would be plenty of room for Bert and Nan to cuddle up and get what sleep they could on the back seats. Luckily there was a robe on the rail in the rear, and this could be put over the children to keep them warm. For, though it was almost summer, the nights were still cool.

"And I'll put up the side curtains," decided Mr. Bobbsey.

"Where will you sleep?" asked Bert.

"Oh, I'll curl up on the front seat. It won't be the first time I've been out all night in an auto," laughed Mr. Bobbsey.

With the side curtains on the car it really was snug and comfortable, and they would be protected even in the case of rain. But they could catch glimpses of the stars and did not think there would be a storm.

"Now for our supper!" cried Mr. Bobbsey cheerfully.

He divided the sandwiches, giving Nan and Bert the most, and the bottles of soda water were opened.

"I've a cake of chocolate, too," said Bert, fishing up a square of milk chocolate from one pocket.

Night now settled down over the woods where the Bobbsey twins—at least, half of them—were lost. They ate and drank and then, curled up on the back seat, Nan and Bert listened to stories their father told them.

At first the children asked questions or made comments as the stories were told. But, after a while, Mr. Bobbsey noticed that the questions were shorter and farther apart. Soon he heard Bert and Nan breathing heavily.

"I believe they're asleep," he said softly.

He looked back, and, by the light of the dashboard lamp, he saw the twins slumbering. Mr. Bobbsey pulled the robe over them. Then, making himself as comfortable as he could in the front seat, he prepared to pass the night. He did not at once fall asleep, for he was thinking of many things.

"Queer how I got on the wrong road—for that's what I must have done," he mused. "And it's queer that the old woman in the faded shawl would come up this lonely road. I wonder who she is? I wonder why she deserted Baby May?"

He could find no answers to these questions, so, after a while, he began to doze off. Before he knew it his eyes were closing, and he was slumbering.

But it was not for long. Suddenly he sat up, he felt the auto jar, as though some one had brushed against it, or had tried to get in. Instantly Mr. Bobbsey was awake and sitting up.

"Who's there?" demanded Mr. Bobbsey, in a whisper, for he did not want to awaken Nan and Bert, who were still sleeping.

There was no answer, so he turned on the bright headlights of the car. As he did so there was a scurrying in the underbrush, and in the powerful gleam of the lamps he saw a small animal scurrying away amid the trees.

"A fox or a stray dog," decided Mr. Bobbsey. "It must have knocked against the wheel and jarred me awake. It's just as well the children don't know it."

He turned off the lights and again composed himself to sleep. He was dreaming that he was trying to catch the big frog in the spring of the queer woman when, through his dream, he seemed to hear a voice saying:

"Daddy! Daddy, wake up! I hear a noise!"

Mr. Bobbsey sat up with a start, to find Nan leaning over the back of the front seat and gently shaking him by the shoulder.

"Eh? What's the matter?" murmured Mr. Bobbsey, sleepily.

"I—I heard a noise!" whispered Nan. "Listen!"

Faintly, through the darkness of the night, came a crackling sound, as though some large animal was approaching the car.

CHAPTER XII

RESCUED

"WHAT is it, Daddy?" asked Bert, who had also been awakened, more by Nan's voice than by the noise in the night. "What is it?" he inquired again.

"Nan heard something. I guess we can all hear it now," answered Mr. Bobbsey, as the sound of breaking twigs, branches and underbrush told of some large body advancing.

"Do you think it could be a—bear?" faltered Nan.

"Of course not," laughed her father. "There are no bears in these woods. It may be another auto coming, breaking its way along a narrow road."

"It sounds more like one of those war tanks we saw in the soldiers' parade, Nan," remarked Bert. "It's coming over everything."

And, truly, this seemed to be the case. Whoever or whatever it was, drew on crashingly. Nearer and nearer to the automobile came the loud sounds. Nan was almost ready to scream. Mr. Bobbsey had turned on the head-lights again, but nothing showed directly in front of their glare.

Then, suddenly, Bert gave a yell and leaped to Nan's side of the car.

"Oh! It's coming into the auto!" he cried.

Nan looked through the celluloid windows of the side curtains and saw, in the gleam of the little light on the dash, the head and face of what, at first, she took to be a monster animal.

She opened her mouth to scream, but her father caught sight of the animal at the same time, and he gave a loud laugh. This kept Nan from screaming, and also made Bert turn around to look.

"It's only a horse!" cried Mr. Bobbsey. "A wandering horse. It has been crashing its way through the underbrush, and now it has come to see what we are doing here, I suppose."

"Oh! Only a horse!" faltered Nan, some-what ashamed of her needless fear.

"Just old Dobbin, the horse!" chuckled her father.

"He made noise enough for a whole circus," declared Bert. "And when I saw him looking in through the curtain I thought—well, crickity grasshoppers, I didn't know what to think."

"I'm glad the horse came along," said Mr. Bobbsey, as the animal, after sniffing at the automobile once or twice, continued on his wandering way, crashing through the masses of underbrush in the darkness.

"Well, I'm not," declared Nan. "He frightened me."

"Why are you glad about the horse, Daddy?" asked Bert.

"Because it shows there must be a farm near here, and we'll find our way out in the morning," was the answer.

"I hope so," murmured Nan.

"Better go to sleep again," suggested her father. "And don't be frightened by any more noises. Noise can't harm you, and there are no bears or other wild beasts in these woods."

Nan and Bert curled up again, and were soon sound asleep, though their bed was not

the most comfortable one they might have had.
But being young and tired, they soon fell into
a sound, healthy slumber.

Once again during the night Nan heard a
noise. It was the distant hooting of an owl,
who kept inquiring:

Who? Who? Who?

But Nan had heard owls before and knew
what they were. So she paid little attention
to this one, and was soon asleep again.

Mr. Bobbsey, however, was not so lucky.
He nearly dozed off once or twice, but when he
got to thinking of all that had happened during
the day—the chase after the strange woman
with the faded shawl, the old woman with the
big frog, and how he had taken the wrong
road and so become lost—it excited him a little
and kept him awake.

"And I do hope the folks at home aren't
worrying too much," thought Mr. Bobbsey.
He knew his wife would worry a little—that
could not be helped. He felt that she knew
he would have sent word to her had it been
possible. However, there was no telephone
in the woods, but he made up his mind to talk

to her as soon as possible in the morning—calling her up from the first telephone he reached.

In truth, Mrs. Bobbsey did worry some. But she felt that the children were safe with their father, and she knew her husband would have sent word had he been able. Baby May was somewhat troublesome, on account of cutting a tooth, and this kept Mrs. Bobbsey rather busy all night.

In the woods hours of darkness passed, and at last those waiting in the automobile saw another day coming. At least, Mr. Bobbsey noticed the growing light in the east. Nan and Bert were still sound asleep.

"I guess I'll get out and stretch my legs—I'm all cramped up," said Mr. Bobbsey to himself, when it grew a little lighter. "We'll soon start and see where we come out."

He slipped quietly from the car so as not to awaken Nan and Bert, and, walking a little way down the woodland road, he saw a spring of water. There he washed his hands and face, and felt much refreshed. He also took a long drink.

"Not much of a breakfast, but it will have to do," chuckled Mr. Bobbsey. "I feel sorry for the children, though."

However, Nan and Bert thought it rather jolly fun. When they awakened they, too, washed and drank at the spring, and then Bert brought out his cake of milk chocolate.

"Nan, you set the table and I'll get breakfast," he jokingly said. And Nan, joining in the joke, put three broad green leaves for plates on a flat stump.

"Now we'll eat," said Bert.

He was about to break the chocolate into three pieces, but his father said:

"None for me, Bert, thank you. I never could eat sweet stuff so early in the morning. You two eat it all and then we'll start for home, if we can find the way."

The boy broke the chocolate into two pieces, giving the larger one to Nan, for which she thanked him. She was very fond of chocolate, even in the morning. For that matter, so was Bert, and I give him credit for being unselfish. Not that he wasn't a "regular boy." Indeed, he had his faults—he wouldn't have been a boy if he hadn't had some. But he was of a generous nature.

"Please take a little bite of my breakfast, Daddy," begged Nan, as she nibbled her chocolate.

"I really don't want it," her father said. But she prevailed on him to take a nibble, and so did Bert.

It did not take long to finish "breakfast," and then Mr. Bobbsey started the automobile, which did not balk, refuse to go, or anything like that.

"Which way are you going, Daddy?" asked Bert, as he and his sister took their seats again.

"I don't know that it makes much difference," Mr. Bobbsey replied. "But I think I'll travel back and see if we can get on the road we first took. This big rock doesn't seem to be the right one. We must have turned off the road on which we were traveling, some distance back."

On they chugged through the forest, but it was with lighter hearts now—hearts that were lightened by the smiling sun even as the dark woods were made less gloomy. They would certainly get out of the forest soon, they felt.

However, look about him as Mr. Bobbsey did, he could not tell where the main road was—at least, the road by which he had entered the forest in search of the strange woman.

He saw several wood roads leading off the one which he had traveled, and he tried to tell, by looking at the marks of automobile wheels, which was the way they had originally taken. But other cars had also gone over the same road, so the marks of the wheels of the Bobbsey car could not be picked out.

The twins' father was about to decide to turn about and go the other way when suddenly, from just ahead of them, came a voice, shouting:

"Whoa there! Where you tryin' to go? You've been out all night, an' now you want to run away ag'in! Whoa, I tell you!"

"Sounds like somebody talking to a horse," observed Bert.

"Maybe it was the horse that tried to get into our auto," suggested Nan.

Then, around a bend in the road, came a lanky farmer boy, of not more than fourteen, leading a horse. Whether it was the same animal that had frightened Nan and Bert could not be said for certain at once, though, later, they learned that it was.

The boy, leading the horse, advanced toward the automobile, which Mr. Bobbsey had stopped.

"Mornin', neighbors," called the youth pleasantly and not at all bashfully. "You're out early."

"I might say the same of you," remarked Mr. Bobbsey. "We've been out all night— lost in the woods. Can you put me on the road to Hankertown?"

"Straight ahead and take the first turn to the left," said the lad. "You're on the old lumber road that isn't used much any more. This horse seems to like it, for he ran away last night and I only just found him."

"I think we found him first," said Mr. Bobbsey, and he described the visit of the animal in the night.

"I reckon that was our horse," the boy said.

"It's just like old Jim to go pokin' his nose in where he isn't wanted. Hope he didn't do any damage."

"Not any," laughed Mr. Bobbsey. "And I'm much obliged to you for setting us right. I got all mixed up on these wood roads. Is there any restaurant or eating place before I get to Hankertown?"

"Restaurant? Good land, no! But say! ain't you folks had any breakfast?" he demanded.

"Not yet," said Mr. Bobbsey.

"Well, neither have I, but I reckon on havin' some right soon. Our house is only about a mile back, on another road. If you want to go there my mother'll be glad to give you something hot."

"I wouldn't want to trouble her," objected Mr. Bobbsey.

"No trouble at all. She likes to have folks to meals. Say, I believe I could sit on the back of your machine and lead old Jim along by his halter, if you didn't go too fast. Then I could be right there with you and explain."

"Thank you, I wish you would," replied Mr.

Bobbsey.   And the farmer boy was soon sitting on the back seat, between Nan and Bert, while, following behind, led by the long halter, was Jim, the midnight-wandering horse.

"There's our place," said Silas Remington, which proved to be the name of the farmer boy.   "Drive right up.   My mother'll be s'prised to see me comin' back in style, I reckon," and he chuckled as he pointed out a small house set in a little clearing of the woods.

CHAPTER XIII

THE LAST DAY

"For the land sakes, Silas! what happened? Did ye break your leg?"

This was what Mrs. Remington asked as she saw her son driving up in the automobile to the little house in the clearing, leading the strayed horse by the halter from the back seat.

"There has been no accident," said Mr. Bobbsey quickly, for he did not want the boy's mother to worry. "We just met your son and gave him a ride home, and—"

"These folks have been out in the woods all night, Mother!" Silas Remington explained. "I found them when I was hunting old Jim down the wood road. Now if you can give them some breakfast—"

"I'm sure we don't want to trouble you," interrupted Mr. Bobbsey. "But I'd be glad to pay—"

"Pay! Nonsense! No trouble at all! Come right in, and I'll have breakfast ready in a jiffy!" exclaimed the kind Mrs. Remington. "You take the horse to the barn, Silas, and then come in and get your breakfast, and bring your pa with you. Silas started out early to find Jim," she explained to the Bobbseys, as she bustled about.

"It's a good thing for us that he did," said Mr. Bobbsey, "or I don't know how much longer we might have been wandering in the woods. But where can I get a telephone? I must let my wife know we are all right—she'll be worried."

"We've got a telephone," said Mrs. Remington. "I don't bother with it much myself, but my husband thought he had to have one. Next I know he'll be gettin' a tin Lizzie, I guess," and she laughed.

Mr. Bobbsey was soon talking to his wife over the telephone, while the farmer's wife was getting breakfast.

"Oh, I'm so glad you're all right!" exclaimed Mrs. Bobbsey, when she heard her husband's voice. "I couldn't imagine what had happened, but I knew the children would be all right with you. How's Baby May? Oh, she's fine, and she's cut another tooth! That's why she fretted so last night!"

Bert and Nan were glad to know all were well at home, and then they sat down to a good breakfast. All their troubles were over now, for Mr. Remington, who had come into breakfast with Silas and who had a small farm on the edge of the woods, told Mr. Bobbsey where to drive to get back to the main road to Hankertown.

"But about that strange old woman with the faded shawl you were after, I don't know," and the farmer shook his head. "I never seen her around these parts. She must be a stranger here."

"Could it have been old Mary Dodd back by the spring?" asked Mrs. Remington. "She's very odd."

"You mean the woman with the frog in the spring?" inquired Mr. Bobbsey. "No, we saw old Mary and she gave us water. The woman I am seeking is another person."

"Wa-all, then I'm afraid I can't help you,"

said Mr. Remington, with a shake of his head. "But if Silas or I see the old woman around I'll try and find out who she is and let you know."

"Sure we will!" piped up Silas.

"I wish you would," returned Mr. Bobbsey, and he prepared to set out again with Nan and Bert in the automobile.

They bade good-bye to the kind farmer and his wife and to his talkative son, and were soon out of the woods and on the main highway. Mr. Bobbsey did not think it would be of any use to try further to locate the strange woman, so he drove directly back to Lakeport.

"My, you had an adventure, didn't you?" exclaimed Mrs. Bobbsey, when the twins and their father arrived.

"I should say we did!" ejaculated Nan.

"But it was jolly fun!" laughed Bert. "Even when the horse tried to stick his head in through the side curtains."

"Tell me about it!" begged Freddie.

"I want to hear, too," said Flossie. "And Baby May has a new tooth—she has!"

"Yes, we heard about that over the telephone," laughed Nan.

The smaller twins were delighted to hear the account of the adventures of Nan and Bert in the night, and Freddie declared that the next time his father went on a trip like that he was going too.

"Well, so you didn't find the old woman after all?" remarked Mrs. Bobbsey, after she had talked matters over quietly with her husband.

"No. And it begins to look as if we never should. She is more of a mystery than ever. I have notified the police of Hankertown, though, and they said they would keep a lookout for her."

"And until she is found and tells us the secret of baby May, we will keep the little girl," suggested Mrs. Bobbsey.

"Wouldn't you rather send her to an orphan asylum?" asked Mr. Bobbsey, thinking perhaps the care of the baby was too much for his wife.

"Oh, no indeed!" she exclaimed. "I never

could give her up now, unless it were to her real mother."

"I'd like to know where the real mother is," said Mr. Bobbsey. "It certainly seems very strange!"

Baby May did not seem to mind being the center of a mystery. She grew fatter and taller, her eyes seemed bluer, her hair more golden, and certainly her smile was sweeter. She was a dear little baby, and every one loved her, especially the Bobbsey twins.

Summer was close at hand now. Every day it seemed warmer and warmer to have to go to school. With the windows open, so the sweet wind blew in and the songs of birds could be heard, it was quite a task to keep the children at their lessons. Miss Riker found it so in the room where Bert and Nan recited.

"Well, children," said the teacher one Monday afternoon, as the class was about to leave for the day, "Friday, you know, is the last day of school for the term."

The girls looked at one another with glad eyes, and the boys wanted to shout, but that would not have been allowed. So they kept quiet, though it was hard work.

"We will have some exercises in our room for the last day," went on Miss Riker, "and those who wish to may recite a piece or sing. We will make up a program. There will be no lessons, but just some exercises. Now, those of you who wish to recite will please tell me the name of their piece after school. Now you may go!"

There was a buzz of excitement, all the boys and girls talking about the joyous "last day" of school.

Examinations were over, Nan and Bert successfully "passed," as did most of their chums, and Freddie and Flossie proudly brought home their report cards, showing that they had done well and could be advanced to a higher class next term.

"I'm going to speak that piece about the Indian Chief," announced Bert, as the last day drew near.

"And I'm going to sing a duet with Nellie Parks," said Nan.

The two children were practicing hard to

have their numbers a success when they got up before the class on the last day of school.

There was in Bert's class a boy named Sam Todd. He was a pretty good boy—sometimes; but he was very fond of playing tricks or jokes—on others, you must know. Bert didn't remember that he ever played a trick or joke on himself, though.

Sam had heard about the piece Bert was going to speak, and just before the last day, Sam said to his chum, Joe Norton:

"I'm going to play a good joke when Bert Bobbsey gets up to speak his piece."

"What are you goin' to do?" Joe asked.

"Well, I got a lot of turkey feathers and I fastened 'em to an old football. I made it look like the head of an Indian. I made this football-Indian-head fast to a string. I sit right near the window, you know, and when Bert gets up to speak I'm going to pull on the string, and I'll pull it in through the window, the football with feathers on. I'll pull it in just when Bert hollers out that line about: 'What is this fearful thing I see?' In will pop the feathered football, and say—won't there be a howl!"

"Goodness, yes!" gasped Joe. "That's a dandy trick! But are you sure the thing will come in the window when you pull the string?"

"I'll put it outside the window just before we come in for the last day, and I'll tie the string to my desk. It'll be easy for me to pull it in. Oh, boy! Some joke! Eh?"

"Oh, boy! Some joke!" echoed Joe, with a chuckle.

Bert, knowing nothing of this, kept on studying his piece. Finally the last day of school came. There were to be exercises in the different rooms, more simple ones where Flossie and Freddie were.

After Nan and Nellie had sung and other boys and girls had taken their parts, Bert's turn came. He walked rather nervously up to the platform on which stood Miss Riker's desk.

"Now for the joke!" whispered Sam Todd to Joe, who sat in front of him. There was a string running from Sam's desk out of the open window. The other end of the string had been fastened to the old football covered with feathers. At a distance it did look like the head of an Indian.

Bert started his recitation. He got along very well, and at last he came to the line where he had to call, several times, loudly:

"What is this fearful thing I see?"

Just as Bert started this Sam gave a hard pull on the string. He expected to haul in his "trick."

But something had gone wrong!

CHAPTER XIV

A BIG SPLASH

BERT BOBBSEY was speaking his piece so well that his teacher and the other boys and girls did not see what Sam Todd was trying to do. The eyes of all in the room were fixed on Bert—that is, the eyes of all but Sam and his chum Joe. Bert had practiced his recitation many times at home, his mother helping and correcting him, until he could do it very well.

All this mattered nothing to Sam, however, if he could spoil Bert's recitation by playing the trick. With all that, Sam did not intend to be mean. It was all just a "good joke" to him and Joe.

But, as was said, something went wrong.

When Sam pulled on the string it seemed to be caught on something outside the window. The football with its feathers, making it look like the head of an Indian, did not bounce in through the open window, as Sam hoped it would.

There was no time to lose. Bert was just beginning the startling line—

"What is this fearful thing I see?"

If the football did not pop in now the joke would be spoiled. As all eyes were on Bert, Sam felt it would be safe to leave his seat to look and find out what the trouble was. He had a little time, as Bert had to say this line three times—slowly.

Bert gave the line once. He paused. He repeated it. Sam was now leaning over the edge of the window sill, looking down to see what was holding the string of the feather-decorated football.

Then Bert exclaimed, very loudly:

"What is this fearful thing I see?"

As he did so, Sam Todd lost his balance and fell out of the window. But that was not all! Just under the window was a big barrel of water, that had been used by masons when they had done some work on the school foundation.

With a splash and a cry of surprise, Sam Todd toppled into this barrel of water, his shout of alarm mingling with Bert's dramatic demand to know what fearful thing it was that he saw.

"Oh, dear, look at that!"

"Sammie's out of the window!"

"He's in the water!"

"He'll be drowned!"

"What was he doing anyway?"

And so the cries of the children ran on.

Well, of course that brought Bert's recitation to a sudden end. No boy could speak a piece with another lad falling out of the window into a barrel of water and yelling at the same time.

"What is it? What has happened?" exclaimed Miss Riker, leaping to her feet.

"Sammie Todd fell out of the window," answered Sadie Moore, who was a quick little thing.

"What in the world was he doing? Why was he leaning out of the window in that way?" demanded Miss Riker; for she had seen Sam at the sill just before he fell.

"He wanted to—he was going to—" began Joe Norton. Then Joe happened to think it was hardly the fair thing to tell on Sam—to let the teacher know about the joke. She might find out anyhow—very likely she would—but Joe could not tell.

"What was Sam going to do?" demanded Miss Riker. But no one answered her, and from outside the window sounded the splashing in the barrel of water and the voice of Sam begging for help.

"We must go to him. Maybe he is hurt," the teacher said, starting for the door.

But Bert was ahead of her. He did not much mind having his recitation broken up in this queer way. As a matter of fact, Bert only laughed about it afterward.

But now Sam might be in danger, through his own foolishness, and might need help. So Bert and some of the other boys rushed out of school ahead of the teacher. These boys, too, rather welcomed the interruption. They did not care much about "speaking pieces."

As Bert and his chums reached the school yard under the open window, they saw Sam, dripping wet and covered with bits of lime and plaster, climbing from the barrel of water.

"I—I—now—I fell in!" spluttered Sam, as if there was any need of an explanation. "I—I—now—fell right in!"

"I should say you did!" laughed Bert. He could laugh now, and so could the other boys, for Sam was not in the least hurt.

Sam balanced himself for a moment on the edge of the barrel and then slipped down and out, over the edge. The water ran from him and made little puddles around his feet.

"How did it happen? Are you sure you aren't hurt?" asked Miss Riker.

Sam did not answer the first question, but to the second he replied.

"Oh, no'm—thank you—I'm not hurt. I—I'm just—wet!"

"Yes, we see you are," observed Miss Riker, trying not to smile, for by this time she began to suspect that something was wrong. No boy sitting in his seat in a quiet schoolroom, where "speaking pieces" is going on, can fall out of the window and into a barrel of water without having done something himself to bring it about.

Once it was certain that Sam had suffered no more than a wetting, the teacher began to cast about to find an explanation. Her quick eye caught sight of the string running in through the open window to the schoolroom. Stepping to the window she looked inside and saw that the string was fastened to Sam's desk.

Another look, on the ground near the barrel, disclosed the football and the feathers on it. Then she understood.

"Oh, I see," she murmured. "This was a sort of—joke, Sam? Was that it?"

"Ye—ye—yes'm," faltered the dripping lad.

"Very well. You may go back to your seats, children—that is, all but Sam. You had better go home and change into dry clothes," she added, and this time she smiled broadly.

"Shall I—now—shall I come back?" asked Sam. All the joking spirit had departed.

"No, you don't need to come back," said Miss Riker. "School will be out for the term by the time you could return." And as Sam, rather shame-faced, made his dripping way toward his home, the teacher remarked: "I hardly think it worth while to go on with the closing exercises. They were almost finished, anyhow. Unless, Bert, you wish to conclude your recitation?" she added, turning to the Bobbsey twin questioningly.

"Oh, no'm—thank you—I don't mind quitting!" Bert made haste to say. He did not exactly object to "speaking pieces," but if there was a good excuse to get out of it, he was glad of that excuse. "I can recite it next term," he added.

"Yes, I suppose so," returned Miss Riker, with a laugh. "Well, boys and girls, you may go now. School is over for the term. I hope you'll all have a happy vacation."

"Thank you! Thank you! The same to you!" chorused the boys and girls.

There were murmurs, talks, laughter and a general movement of relief. No more books or studies for more than two months—oh, joy!

Some of the pupils returned to the classroom

to get things from their desks. Charlie Mason was beside Bert as the two boys walked over to the water barrel to look more closely at the "joke."

"Say, Bert, I'm glad you said you didn't care about going on with your piece," said Charlie.

"Why?" asked Bert.

" 'Cause I was after you, and I didn't know my piece very well. There's one verse I never can remember, and I know I'd have broken down up on the platform. So I'm glad I didn't have to speak."

"So'm I," murmured Bert. "Say, what is that thing, anyhow?" he asked, as Joe Norton pulled into view the "joke" Sam Todd had prepared with such care.

"Looks like a scalped Indian," remarked Danny Rugg.

"That's what Sam made it for," chuckled Joe. "He was going to pull it in when you said that line, Bert, about what a fearful thing you saw."

"Ha! Ha!" laughed Bert. "He was going

to pull it in, was he? Well, he pulled himself *out* instead! It was a good joke all right!"

And so it was, only it turned just the other way from what Sam intended. But very often jokes do turn that way.

However, nothing much now mattered except that school was out for the long vacation.

"Where are you going for your vacation?" asked May Miller of Nan Bobbsey, as she walked home with Flossie and Freddie. Bert had gone on ahead with some of the boys.

"We don't exactly know," Nan replied. "Since we have Baby May with us, mother and daddy haven't made up their minds. I guess we'll go away somewhere."

"We're going to the seashore," said May.

"We've been there—lots of times," Nan said.

"I like the seashore!" murmured Flossie. "We went there and played in the sand."

"And Flossie fell into the water!" added Freddie, anxious to tell all the news.

"So did you fall in, too!" countered Flossie.

"Yes, we both fell in!" laughed her twin

brother, shaking his head of golden hair. "It was lots of fun."

"Well, I want to go swimming in the ocean," said May, laughing at the smaller Bobbsey twins, "but I don't exactly want to fall in. I suppose Baby May is too young to be taken to the seashore," she added, for by this time every one in Lakeport knew about the little foundling who had been left on the Bobbsey doorstep.

"Yes, I suppose so," agreed Nan. "But we'll go away somewhere, I'm sure. Good-bye, May!"

"Good-bye," May answered, as she turned down her street.

"I'm going to ask mother if I can wheel Baby May out in the baby carriage," said Flossie, as she and her sister and brother neared home.

"You'll have to be very careful, and stay right in front of the house," cautioned Nan. "We don't want any more runaways."

"I'll be careful," promised Flossie.

But when they reached the house and went clattering up the steps, Mrs. Bobbsey came softly out of the door with a hand raised to stop them.

"Hush!" she whispered. "Don't make any noise!"

"What's the matter?" asked Nan, in a low voice.

"Baby May is sick," Mrs. Bobbsey replied. "The doctor has been here, and the poor little thing has just gone to sleep. Don't make any noise!"

CHAPTER XV

FREDDIE SEES SOMETHING

WITH hushed voices and walking on tip-
toes, the smaller Bobbsey twins and Nan entered the house. Mrs. Bobbsey closed the door
softly after them.

"Where is she? Where is Baby May?"
asked Flossie.

"May I look at her?" asked Freddie soberly.

"Not now, dears," their mother answered.
"She has just fallen asleep, and I don't want
her to awaken. You may see her after she
has had her nap—that is, if she is well
enough."

"Is she very sick?" Nan wanted to know.
"It must have come on suddenly, for she was
all right when we went to school this morning."

"Yes, it was sudden," Mrs. Bobbsey answered. "She was taken with a spasm after

you left, and I had to telephone for the doctor."

"What did he say?" Nan asked, while Flossie and Freddie, hardly breathing so anxious were they to make no noise, waited for the answer.

"He said he thought it was something she had eaten, and he gave me some medicine for her. After she took it she fell asleep. She is up in my room now."

"Is anybody with her?" asked Nan. "We got out of school a little earlier on account of Bert speaking his piece."

"Dinah is sitting beside Baby May," said Mrs. Bobbsey. "But what do you mean about getting out earlier on account of Bert speaking his piece? I hope he didn't fail or cut up or—"

"Oh, no, *he* was all right," softly laughed Nan. "It was Sammie Todd. He fell out of the window—"

"Fell out of the window!" exclaimed Mrs. Bobbsey, and then she suddenly lowered her voice for fear of waking Baby May. "Was he hurt?" she whispered.

"No," chuckled Nan, and then she told what

had happened. "I'll go up and sit by the baby," she added, when she had finished the story.

"All right, then Dinah can come down," Mrs. Bobbsey said. "You and Flossie go out and play, Freddie," she added to the younger twins. "But don't make any noise."

"I'll play with my paper dolls—they don't make a sound," decided Flossie.

"And I'll take my little cart with the rubber tires on the wheels—that doesn't make any noise, either," said Freddie.

"Why can't you give my family a ride in the cart?" suggested Flossie. "The children haven't had a ride for a long time." By children, she of course meant her paper dolls.

"I'll tell you what I'll do," answered Freddie. "We'll pretend the cart is a trolley car and the children can ride on it. Only they have to pay fare. Little stones will do for money."

And so it was arranged.

With the younger twins thus safely amusing themselves, Nan could spend her time with the baby.

She went quietly up to the room where

Dinah sat beside the bed on which little May was lying.

"De honey lamb is gettin' bettah," whispered Dinah. "I kin tell by de way she breeves. Dat doctor man's medicine done her a powerful sight ob good! But don't wake her up. Let her sleep! Sleep's de best when a baby's sick."

"Yes," agreed Nan, in a whisper, and then she sat silent beside the bed.

Baby May was a beautiful picture to look upon as she slept—a beautiful picture, but just a little sad, Nan thought. For the little child seemed friendless and alone in the world, no one, seemingly, knowing where her father and mother were. No one ever to have cared for her save the queer old woman with the green umbrella!

"I wonder where that woman is now," thought Nan, as she listened to the breathing of Baby May. As Dinah had said, her "breeves" were quieter, now that the medicine had its effect. But she still looked ill, Nan thought, as she tenderly touched one dimpled hand with a finger.

Outside in the yard below the bedroom window. Flossie and Freddie could be heard at their play. They made only a little noise—not enough to waken the baby. Nan heard them and smiled, then she almost laughed as she thought of how Sam had fallen into the barrel of water.

The baby stirred uneasily in her sleep and cried faintly. Mrs. Bobbsey came quickly up the stairs and appeared in the room.

"If she is waking I must give her some more medicine," she said.

Baby May awoke with a pitiful, fretful sick cry, and she wailed more loudly as she became more widely awake. It was hard work to make her take the medicine, but at least she swallowed some, and then she cried harder than ever.

"Poor little dear!" murmured Nan. "She must be terribly sick!"

"Oh, perhaps not," said Mrs. Bobbsey. "Little babies cry very hard for only a slight illness. The doctor did not seem to think it was anything serious. But he is coming in again."

"Shall I take her out in the carriage?" offered Nan.

"Oh, no. She must stay in the house," her mother answered.

Flossie and Freddie came creeping up the stairs, having left their play at the sound of the baby's cries.

"Is she all right now?" asked Flossie. "Could I take her out?"

"She is far from being all right," answered Mrs. Bobbsey. "Better run down and play some more, little twins. Nan and I will look after Baby May."

"She sounds all right," observed Freddie. "She's making a lot of noise," for the infant was crying hard.

"All babies have to cry," wisely remarked Flossie, as she went downstairs with her brother. "You cried when you were little."

"I don't 'member it," said Freddie.

The doctor came again that evening soon after supper. He carefully looked the baby over and, after sitting in his chair and appearing to be in deep thought, he asked:

"Has she ever had the jaundice?"

"I don't know," Mrs. Bobbsey answered. "You see, she isn't our baby, exactly. She was left on our doorstep, and what she may have had and gotten over I don't know."

"Um—yes," remarked the doctor. "Well, it looks to me as if she were going to have a touch of the jaundice; she's getting a bit yellow. I'll give her some new medicine," and he began to write on one of his prescription blanks.

"What's jaundice, Mother?" asked Nan, when the doctor was gone. "Did I ever have it?"

"Yes, you had it, and you turned as yellow as saffron, so Dinah said. As a rule, it isn't anything serious. Little babies often have it. Their stomachs get out of order. But I will need to have this medicine brought from the drug store."

"I'll get it," offered Bert.

"I'll go with you," said Nan.

"We'll go, too," chimed in Flossie and Freddie.

"No, it's too late," said their father, for,

though it was not yet dark, night was fast coming on.

However, it was not too late for Bert and Nan to go to the drug store, which was only a few blocks away, and out they started. Bert had some money saved up, and he treated his sister to an ice-cream cone while they waited for the medicine to be prepared.

It was when the twins were on their way home that Bert saw Nan stop, turn around, and look back several times.

"What's the matter?" he finally asked.

"I thought I saw some one following us," she answered.

"Some one coming after us, do you mean?"

"Yes."

"Who was it—Danny Rugg?" asked Bert. "He isn't mean any more. He used to follow you and throw stones at you, but he doesn't any more."

"No, it wasn't Danny Rugg," Nan answered.

"Who then?"

"It was an old woman."

"An old woman!" exclaimed Bert. "Do

you mean it was the same one who left Baby May?"

"I couldn't be sure about that," replied Nan, once more glancing back over her shoulder. "But it was some old woman. She has been following us for two blocks."

"Wait a minute—we'll fool her the way detectives do!" exclaimed Bert, not explaining how he happened to know anything about detectives.

"What you going to do?" asked Nan.

"We'll turn the next corner, and then we'll hide in a doorway," Bert explained. "If any old woman is following us she'll think we kept right on and we can see who she is."

"Oh, I know, like playing tag," said Nan.

So the children turned the next corner quickly, and then, swinging back, hid themselves in a doorway. They waited, but no one followed them. They waited some little time longer. Then Bert stepped out and looked back down the street from which they had turned.

"No one's coming," he said. "I guess you didn't see anybody, Nan."

"Yes, I did," she insisted.

When the twins reached home with the medicine, and told their parents about the matter, Mr. Bobbsey said:

"I don't believe it was the same old woman. She doesn't want to be found out, that's certain; so she wouldn't come back to the same town in which she deserted the baby. It was some other old woman, Nan."

"Well, perhaps it was, Daddy," said Bert's sister.

After that they thought no more about it. The new medicine seemed to be just what Baby May needed, for she was much better the next day. She really had the jaundice, and her skin grew ever so yellow, causing the Bobbsey twins to fear for the worst. But their mother laughed at their alarm and said Baby May would soon be better.

And she was. A few days later she could be taken out in the yard and allowed to sleep in the hammock beneath the overshadowing trees.

Mrs. Bobbsey placed Baby May in the hammock, where the little thing crowed and cooed in her happiness at feeling well again. Freddie was with his mother. Nan had taken Flossie down to a store to buy her a new hair ribbon. Bert had gone fishing with some of the boys.

"De telafoam am ringin'," announced Dinah, coming to the back door and calling to Mrs. Bobbsey. "Somebody done want yo', Mrs. Bobbsey."

"I'll come right in, Dinah. Freddie, you watch Baby May a little while, and don't swing the hammock."

"No'm, I won't," Freddie promised.

He sat beside the baby, smiling at her, for she was so pretty and cute, and letting May catch hold of one of his fingers. Then, as Freddie looked toward the street he saw something—or rather, some one. And that some one was an old lady in a faded shawl. Freddie insisted afterward that the shawl was faded.

At any rate, an old lady passed the Bobbsey house, and when she saw a baby swinging in a hammock in the side yard, with a little boy sitting beside the hammock, a strange look came over her face.

"Oh!" softly murmured Freddie. "Oh, it's the same old woman!"

As he spoke thus to himself the old woman put her hand on the closed gate, and seemed about to push it open.

"Don't come in here! Don't you come in!" screamed Freddie, in such a loud voice that he frightened Baby May and she began to cry.

"Don't you come in!" Freddie shouted again.

CHAPTER XVI

A LOST BABY

VERY much frightened and hardly knowing what he was doing, Freddie sprang toward the hammock and started to take Baby May up in his arms. It was almost more than he could do, for he did not know much about the way to carry babies. But he made up his mind to keep Baby May safe.

Freddie gave one look back over his shoulder as he reached down to take up the infant, and he saw that the old lady, whoever she was, did not intend to come into the yard. She had put her hand on the gate as if to open it, and then she seemed to change her mind.

She was muttering something to herself, but what it was Freddie could not hear.

Again he cried:

"You can't come in here! Go away! You can't have Baby May!"

The old woman turned away without opening the gate, and walked off down the street. Freddie's heart stopped beating so fast.

Mrs. Bobbsey, alarmed by Freddie's screams, came running out of the house after having answered the telephone.

"Freddie, what is the matter?" his mother asked. "You shouldn't take Baby May up out of the hammock!" she went on. "You might drop her. Don't lift her up!"

By this time Freddie had ceased trying to lift Baby May. He let her sink back on the soft blankets in the hammock and, then, turning to his mother, he said:

"I was going to bring her into the house."

"Why, Freddie Bobbsey! What in the world made you do that?" his mother asked. "Didn't I tell you never to try to carry May?"

"I didn't want the old lady to get her!"

"What old lady?" asked Mrs. Bobbsey, though she knew, almost without asking, what person Freddie must mean.

"That same old lady," Freddie replied. "The one with the green umbrella, but she didn't have a green umbrella this time. She had on a faded shawl and—"

"Did she try to come in here and get May?" asked Mrs. Bobbsey, now almost as much excited as Freddie was. "Where is she? Where did she go?"

"She didn't come in," the little boy replied. "But she put her hand on the gate and I yelled and—"

"Yes, I heard you," gasped Mrs. Bobbsey. "But go on—what else happened, Freddie?"

"Nothing, Mother. She just went away—down the street."

Mrs. Bobbsey hastened to the gate and looked up and down the street, but she saw no sign of the curious old woman.

"Are you sure you saw her, Freddie?" she inquired.

"Course I'm sure!" replied Flossie's twin brother. "I saw her with my own eyes, and so did Baby May! You can ask her!" He looked down at the cooing child as if May could answer. But May only smiled up at Freddie, and her smile was very sweet.

"I must telephone daddy about this," de-

cided Mrs. Bobbsey, after another look up
and down the street, without, however, seeing
the strange woman. "If she is back in Lakeport the police should know about it, so they
can try to find out to whom the baby belongs.
I'll telephone daddy."

This she did, and Mr. Bobbsey grew rather
excited when he heard the news. He hurried
home from the office at the lumber dock and
at once began a search of the neighborhood
for the old woman. He inquired of the neighbors and others, but, though some said they
remembered seeing her, they could not tell
where she had gone.

Nor did the police have any better luck, for
though two of them scurried about town, looking for traces of the stranger, she could not
be found.

"Well, this is very strange," said Mr.
Bobbsey that night, when Baby May had gone
to sleep and they were talking over matters
after supper. "At first I thought maybe Freddie might be mistaken."

"You mean that he didn't see any old lady
at all?" asked Bert.

"Yes. I thought perhaps he might have—well, sort of dreamed it," and Mr. Bobbsey smiled at the little boy.

"I didn't dream it!" cried Freddie, very positively. "I saw the old woman, and so did Baby May. Anyhow, I don't dream in the daytime with my eyes open."

"No, I suppose not," agreed his father. "Well, since you saw her, and since others saw her, there is no doubt but that some old lady started to come into our yard. Whether she was the same one the children saw just before Baby May was left on our doorstep— that is another question."

"I'm sure she was!" insisted Freddie. But of course he was a rather small boy, and he might have been mistaken.

"Then the next thing to think about is," said Mr. Bobbsey, "what did the old woman want?"

"She wanted to take Baby May back!" said Nan promptly.

"I guess she's sorry she gave her away," added Bert.

"It's hard to guess a reason for her strange

acts," observed Mr. Bobbsey. "If she wanted to get rid of the baby, why, now, does she want the child back?"

"I don't want to lose Baby May," said Mrs. Bobbsey softly. "I have grown to love her too much. But of course if her real father and mother wanted her I would be glad to give her up. But I don't believe that old woman is her mother. Do you, Daddy?" she asked her husband.

"No," he replied, "I don't. I think there is some mystery here that we don't understand. Though I can't see why we haven't heard some news in some of the papers about a missing or kidnapped baby. It certainly is very strange. But I have decided on one thing. We shall have no more scares such as Freddie had to-day."

"How are you going to stop it?" asked Bert.

"We will go away for a time," answered Mr. Bobbsey.

"Go away!" echoed the Bobbsey twins.

"Yes. On a little vacation trip," went on

Mr. Bobbsey. "We will go to the country, where the old woman can't find us."

"Oh, to the country!" cried Nan, in delight.

"To Meadow Brook?" asked Bert.

"No, we can hardly go as far away as Meadow Brook," said his father. "Though, no doubt, Uncle Daniel would be glad to see us. But I heard to-day of a nice boarding house in a small country town not far away, and we will go there for a vacation trip."

"Oh, goodie!" cried Flossie.

"Have they got cows?" Freddie demanded.

"I guess so," his father answered. "So, Mother, you had better get ready to go and take Baby May with you," he added.

"If they have cows they must have horses," was Freddie's comment. "And if they have horses I'm going to go horseback riding."

"Why must they have horses if they have cows?" Flossie wanted to know.

"Oh, 'cause they always do. When they take the milk to the station they have to carry the cans in a wagon, don't they? And horses have to pull the wagon, don't they?"

"I'll ride in the wagon. I don't want to go on a horse's back," said Flossie.

There were busy times during the next few days, and then came a short but delightful trip to Pine Hill, a little country town where a farmer and his wife took a few boarders during the summer.

The Bobbsey family about filled the place, and there were only two other people as boarders, two old ladies. Mr. and Mrs. Meekin, who kept the boarding house, welcomed the Bobbsey twins, their parents and Baby May.

"Oh, what a sweet child!" exclaimed Mrs. Meekin. "How old is she?"

"I don't know exactly," replied Mrs. Bobbsey.

"You don't?" cried the two old lady boarders, in surprise.

"No. You see May isn't my child. She is a foundling left on our doorstep," explained Mrs. Bobbsey. She thought it best to tell the true story of Baby May. If she did not, one of the twins would be sure to do so.

Another reason for giving out the fact about Baby May was that Mrs. Bobbsey wanted all

in the house to know about the strange old
woman in the faded shawl, so, if by any chance
she should appear at Pine Hill, the alarm
would be given promptly.

"She is a dear, sweet baby, whoever owns
her," said Miss Himson, one of the old lady
boarders.

"Indeed she is!" agreed Miss Jackson, the
other old lady boarder.

Happy were the days the Bobbsey twins
spent at Pine Hill. Not only were there cows,
to Freddie's delight, but there were sheep and
horses, besides ducks and chickens.

Freddie never tired of watching the ducks
swim, and once he fell into a mud puddle as
he tried to fasten a long string to one of the
ducks. The string was tied to a boat Freddie
had made, and he wanted the duck to pull it.
My, you should have seen Freddie after he
fell into the duck pond! Oh, so muddy and
wet!

But the Bobbsey twins had lots of fun, and
Baby May grew fat and rosy-cheeked in those
days spent in the fresh air of the country.

One day Nan was allowed to wheel the baby

in her carriage to a little clump of woods not far from the house. Bert, Flossie and Freddie also went along, and the children took a lunch with them.

The twins had a regular picnic under the trees in the cool, shady grove, and played games, having a lovely time. Baby May went to sleep in her carriage on top of a little hill, covered with slippery pine needles, down which Freddie and Flossie slid. The needles made the hill almost as slippery as snow or ice would have done.

After a while Bert wandered away to see if he could find a place to fish, for he had brought a hook and line and some bait with him. Flossie and Freddie begged Nan to go with them to look for wild flowers.

"All right, I'll go a little way," agreed Nan. "I guess Baby May will be all right asleep in her carriage."

The two girls and Freddie were gone rather longer than they meant to be, and when they returned to the grove where they had left May in the carriage, the carriage and the baby were gone.

"Oh! Oh!" gasped Nan. "Where is May?"

"Maybe Bert came back and wheeled her around 'cause she was crying," suggested Flossie.

"Oh, maybe! I hope so!" murmured Nan.

But when Bert came back a little later, having found no place to fish, he said he had not wheeled away Baby May.

"Then where is she?" gasped Nan, her heart fluttering strangely.

"She—she's lost!" cried Flossie, and then, as the dreadful thought became clearer to her she sobbed: "Baby May is lost!"

CHAPTER XVII

THE GREEN UMBRELLA

CERTAINLY it was very strange—this vanishing of Baby May, carriage and all. What could it mean?

"Oh! Oh!" sobbed Flossie. "What will mother say? It wasn't my fault, was it?" she asked, remembering the time she had left the baby carriage for a moment and it had so nearly rolled under the runaway horses hitched to the coal wagon.

"No, dear, of course it wasn't your fault," replied Nan soothingly. "But where can the baby be? We weren't gone so very long. Bert, are you sure you aren't playing a joke on us?"

"Course I'm not playing a joke!" ejaculated Bert earnestly. "I wouldn't play a joke like this!"

And Nan believed him.

179

"It's that old woman—I know 'tis!" declared Freddie.

"Let's look around," suggested Nan eagerly. "If the old woman did take May away she can't have got very far. Let's look around!"

Standing on top of the little hill, the Bobbsey twins began to look about them for a possible sight of the old woman hurrying away and wheeling Baby May. But they saw no one.

Suddenly Freddie slipped on the pine needles and began sliding down the hill. It was what he and Flossie had done before, to have fun, but now Freddie's slipping was an accident.

"Oh!" he cried as he felt himself going. "Oh, I'm skidding!"

He had heard his father say this while driving the automobile on a wet and slippery pavement.

Freddie slid all the way down to the bottom of the hill. He came to a stop near a clump of bushes—bushes covered with thick, green leaves.

And then, all of a sudden, while Flossie, Bert and Nan stood on the top of the hill, hardly knowing whether or not to laugh at

Freddie, and when they were wondering what dreadful thing might have happened to Baby May, Freddie gave a loud cry.

It was not a cry as if he were hurt. It was, rather, a cry of joy. Then the little fellow yelled:

"I've found her! I've found Baby May! Here's her carriage in the bushes! I've found her!"

You can imagine how swiftly Bert raced down that hill. Nan tried to follow as fast as her twin brother, but she slipped and slid on the pine needles—she "skidded" just as Freddie had done. As for Flossie, she started to run, but she tripped and fell on her face. Then she, too, slid down the remainder of the way on the brown needles.

In this way all four of the Bobbsey twins reached the bottom of the hill. Bert was the first to get to where Freddie sat, pointing his chubby forefinger.

"Where is it?" demanded Bert. "Where's the carriage and Baby May?"

"Right in there!" Freddie answered.

Bert saw the carriage, almost completely

hidden behind a screen of green leaves. At the same time Nan and Flossie saw it.

"Oh," murmured Nan. "Oh, maybe she isn't in the carriage! Maybe the old woman took May out and pushed the carriage down the hill!"

"We'll soon see!" exclaimed Bert.

He dashed into the bushes, pulled aside the branches that almost covered the carriage, and cried:

"She's all right! She's here fast asleep!"

As he spoke, his loud voice awakened the baby, who cooed and gurgled so that the others heard her.

"I'll wheel her out," said Bert, and a moment later Baby May was surrounded by the Bobbsey twins. Everything was all right now —the lost baby had been found.

"Oh, Baby May! Baby May!" cried Nan, gathering the infant up in her arms. "Oh, if that old woman had taken you what would I have done?"

"Maybe the old woman did try to take her," suggested Bert. "She may have come as far as this down the hill, and then she heard us coming and she hid the carriage here."

"Maybe," agreed Nan. And then, as she remembered how she and the two smaller twins had slipped down the pine needle hill she added: "And maybe the carriage rolled down by itself, Bert. I put the brake on, but sometimes it doesn't hold."

"Yes, maybe it did happen that way," Bert admitted. "The carriage could have rolled down the hill, and it could have rolled in behind the bushes and we wouldn't see it until we went down close and looked—as Freddie did. I guess maybe the carriage did roll down by itself. It could slide easy on the pine needles, and it wouldn't wake up Baby May."

Having caught no sight of the strange old woman, the children finally decided it must all have been an accident.

The brakes did not hold very well, as Nan said, and some movement of the baby in her sleep might have started the carriage to rolling. Down the hill it could easily coast and push its way in through the screen of green leaves, the branches springing back into place, thus hiding the carriage from view until Freddie happened to see it.

"Well, I'm glad everything is all right," announced Nan, as they started back for the boarding house. "I wouldn't want to go home without Baby May."

"Nor I," said Flossie.

It was not easy for Nan and Bert to tell their mother what had happened, but they knew they must. They feared she would blame them for being careless, but all Mrs. Bobbsey said was:

"You must be a little more careful. If you knew the brakes on the carriage didn't hold, Nan, you should have blocked the wheels with a stone or a piece of wood. But I'll have daddy fix the brakes." And the next day Mr. Bobbsey tightened the brakes so they would hold better.

Mr. Bobbsey also went to the hill and looked at the place where it was supposed the carriage had rolled down by itself.

"Yes, it could have happened that way," he said to his wife. "But I must make sure the old woman is not sneaking around here. She may have followed us."

"But we didn't tell any of the neighbors where we were going!" exclaimed Mrs. Bobbsey. "Just on that account we didn't tell them —so if the old woman came back and inquired of the neighbors where we had gone, they couldn't say."

"All the same she may have found out and have come here," returned Mr. Bobbsey. "I'll make some inquiries."

But as no one around Pine Hill had seen the stranger, the father of the Bobbsey twins began to feel a little easier in his mind.

"Probably it was just an accident," he said.

The summer days at Pine Hill were happy ones for the Bobbsey twins. They played about in the woods and fields, and Mrs. Bobbsey sometimes went with them, taking Baby May in her carriage. Flossie and Nan had their dolls to play with, and many a little party they made up under the apple trees. There was a big swing, too, in the orchard, and there the twins had fun all day long.

Bert had become very fond of fishing since coming to Pine Hill. There were several small streams in the country round about, and from them he had pulled several good-sized fish that Mrs. Meekin cooked for him.

One day Bert took Freddie off on a fishing trip to a place about a mile from their boarding house. Freddie had a little pole of his own, and Bert promised to bait the hook for him, as Freddie, otherwise, might get it stuck in his fingers.

The boys sat down on the bank of the stream under a shady buttonwood tree, and tossed their baited hooks into the water. Fastened on their lines were bits of cork, painted green.

"When you see your cork bobber go under the water," said Bert to Freddie, "you want to pull in quick."

"Why?" asked Freddie curiously.

" 'Cause why," answered Bert. " 'Cause when your green bobber goes under it means there's a fish on the hook, and you want to pull it in before it gets off."

"Oh," answered Freddie. Then, after a moment, suddenly he cried: "There she goes!" and he jerked up his pole. On the end of his line was a large, wiggling fish.

"Oh, you caught a good one!" cried Bert.

He took Freddie's fish off the hook, and then Bert caught one himself. The boys were having good luck with their fishing. Presently Freddie stood up to "stretch his legs," as he called it. He gave a sudden start and, looking at Bert, exclaimed:

"I just saw it again, Bert! I just saw it!"

"Saw what?" Bert asked, not paying much attention to his brother, for he felt a nibble at his bait. "What did you just see, Freddie?"

"The green umbrella!" whispered the little fellow. "I just saw a green umbrella going along the road," and he pointed to the highway which passed not far from the stream where the two were fishing. "It was a green umbrella, just like that kidnapper woman carried, Bert!"

CHAPTER XVIII

KIDNAPPED

FOR a moment Bert hardly knew whether or not to believe what Freddie said. Of course he knew that his little brother would not tell an untruth, but Freddie might be mistaken. So Bert made up his mind to ask him again what he had said. The fish which had been nibbling at Bert's bait seemed not to like it, and swam away.

"What did you say you saw, Freddie?" asked the older boy.

"I saw—now—I saw that green umbrella!" whispered Freddie, getting up from his seat on the bank and walking over to Bert. "The green umbrella went past in the road—the same kind of a green umbrella the little old woman had when afterward we found the baby on our steps."

Freddie seemed very sure about this. He

was not fooling—Bert could tell that. And the little boy seemed somewhat frightened. Otherwise he would not have whispered and have come over so close to his older brother.

"Maybe you saw a tree waving in the wind —a tree with green leaves on it, Freddie," suggested Bert, to try him. "Or it might have been a bush that you saw."

"No, sir!" insisted Freddie stoutly. "It was a green umbrella."

"Did you see the little old woman, Freddie?"

"No, I didn't see her. But I saw her umbrella—a green one."

"Well, we'll take a look down the road," decided Bert. "I guess we have enough fish, anyhow, and we might as well go home. We can look and see if the old woman is there."

"If she is, you won't let her take me, will you, Bert?"

"Of course not! Don't be silly!"

"But she's a kidnapper—Nan said she was."

"Well, maybe she did kidnap Baby May and then leave her with us; but she wouldn't take a big boy like you."

"If she did," declared Freddie, winding up

his line, "I'd bite her and I'd kick her and I'd scratch her."

"Well, I guess that wouldn't be any too much for a kidnapper," laughed Bert. "But I don't believe we'll see any one, Freddie."

When the two brothers had crossed the field of clover and reached the highway, there was neither a green umbrella nor an old woman in sight—nothing but the dusty road.

"She isn't here," said Bert. "I didn't think there would be anybody."

"But I did see a green umbrella," insisted Freddie. "Maybe if you looked in the dust you could see her feet marks like when you and the other fellows make believe trail Indians and wild game. Take a look, Bert."

"Well, we can look, but I don't believe we'll find anything," the older boy answered.

But when he saw the plain marks of a woman's shoes in the dust at the side of the road, Bert had to admit that there might have been some woman along there. The footprints came on to the highway at a place where a narrow path wound back into the woods, and they showed that the woman, whoever she was, had come out of the clump of trees and had walked along the dusty road.

"There! What'd I tell you?" exclaimed Freddie. "Wasn't an old woman along here with a green umbrella? I saw it!"

"Some woman has been here—that's plain enough," Bert had to say. "But I can't tell by these marks how old she was, and nobody could tell if she had a green umbrella or not."

"If she had an umbrella, and she kept sticking the end down in the dirt like daddy sticks his cane on Sundays, then you could tell," said Freddie.

"Yes," admitted Bert, "then you could tell. But I don't see any umbrella marks."

Neither could Freddie, but he was sure he had seen the green umbrella passing along the highway. But it had been held up, and the old woman was probably using it as a sunshade; so Freddie had to admit that it could not have made marks in the dust.

The boys followed the trail of the woman's footsteps in the dust as far as they could see them. Then the woman, whoever she was, had stepped from the side of the highway, where the dust was thickest, into the hard, middle part, where there were many wheel marks, both of automobiles and wagons, and also the prints of horses' feet.

"We've lost 'em!" announced Bert, as the footprints vanished. "No use trailing her any farther."

"Can't you tell which way she went?" asked Freddie.

"No," his brother replied. "Maybe she turned around and walked back, or maybe she kept on, and, if she did, she might have turned off on any cross road. No use following her any farther, Freddie."

"All right. But we'll tell daddy and mother, sha'n't we?"

"Oh, sure!" Bert agreed.

The boys trudged back to the house with their strings of fish.

"Oh, what fine luck you had!" cried Nan, as she met them.

"And we had an adventure, too!" burst out Freddie. "I saw the old woman kidnapper—I mean, I didn't *zactly* see her, but I saw her green umbrella and—and—"

But he had to stop, for he was out of breath.

"What does he mean, Bert?" asked Mrs. Bobbsey, with a quick look at her older son.

"Well, he surely thinks he saw the green umbrella," Bert explained, and then he went on with the story.

Mr. Bobbsey looked a bit serious when, later, he heard all about it.

"What do you think?" his wife asked him.

"Of course that strange old woman may have followed us here, and she may be anxious to get Baby May back," said Mr. Bobbsey. "Though how she found us I don't know. And I can't imagine why she is so mysterious. If she wanted the baby, why did she desert her in a storm on our steps? And if she gave her away, why, now, does she want her back?"

"It's all very mysteriousness, isn't it?" asked Nan, and when Bert laughed at her for saying the big word wrong she wrinkled up her nose at him, which was as near as Nan ever came to "making a face."

"Yes, it is strange," her father said, and he did not even smile at Nan's error. "I think I must make some more inquiries around here.

Surely if there is a mysterious woman going about and carrying a green umbrella, some one ought to see her. Meanwhile, you had better take extra good care of Baby May."

"I certainly will do that!" said Mrs. Bobbsey.

For the next few days Baby May was not wheeled in her carriage very far from the house. Or, if she was, either Mr. or Mrs. Bobbsey went with the children who took May out for an airing. Neither Flossie nor Freddie, together or singly, were allowed to wheel Baby May now, unless Bert or Nan went along.

"We can't take any chances," said Mrs. Bobbsey. "Of course May isn't our baby, but I love her as much as though she were, and I don't intend that some one who has no right to her shall take her away from us."

So Baby May was given extra care. She seemed to have gotten all over her illness and laughed and cooed and "talked" for she could now say a few words, though of course she could not put them together in a sentence. She smiled and made her blue eyes sparkle, until Nan, hugging and kissing her, declared she was the "dearest, sweetest and loveliest baby in all the world." And of course she was— just as every baby is to those who love children.

Meanwhile Mr. Bobbsey rode about in his automobile, sometimes taking Nan and Bert with him, and he made inquiries of all whom he met about the mysterious old woman with the green umbrella.

At first he could learn no news. No one seemed to have seen her. But one day, when Mr. Bobbsey and Nan and Bert stopped at a lonely farmhouse so the children could get a drink of water, he got a "clew," as he called it. Afterward he told Bert and Nan that a "clew" on a ship was something to which a rope may be fastened.

"And when you are searching for some one or something, a clew is a bit of information to which you may fasten other news and so, after a while, get enough clews to lead you to what you are looking for," said Mr. Bobbsey.

"Let's see now—a queer old woman with a green umbrella," musingly repeated a farmer of whom Mr. Bobbsey asked this question.

"Yes, I did see such a person. She came to our door four or five days ago and asked for a drink of milk. My wife gave her a glass. I'll call her. She can tell you more than I can."

Mrs. Kenton said that she had seen the queer old woman.

"She carried a faded green umbrella, and she wore a faded shawl," she said to Mr. Bobbsey. "She acted queer, too, and kept putting her hand to her head as if it hurt her. I asked her if it ached and if she didn't want a cup of tea to cure it. But she said it wasn't exactly an ache, but a sort of buzzing. It was getting better she told me, after she had taken the milk."

"Did she say anything about having lost a baby or of having left one on the steps of our house?" asked Mr. Bobbsey.

"Good land! Left a baby on your steps! No, she didn't say anything about that!" exclaimed Mrs. Kenton. "Do tell! Land sakes!"

"I am anxious to know why she is acting so strangely around here," went on Mr. Bobbsey. "Do you know where she lives?"

This the Kentons did not know. The old woman had departed, green umbrella, faded shawl and all, after resting herself and drinking the milk.

"Well, at least we have proved that she is real," said Mr. Bobbsey to Bert and Nan, on their way home. "She isn't imaginary."

"Do you think Freddie saw her?" asked Nan.

"He may have," admitted her father. "I wish I knew what to do about it. I don't want to keep Baby May away from her parents, but I don't want this queer old woman to have her."

Mrs. Bobbsey was a bit excited when she heard the news her husband brought.

"Here, Nan," she said to her daughter, "you take Baby May out in the side yard under the trees with Flossie and Freddie. I want to talk to your father undisturbed for a little while."

Bert had gone with Mr. Meekin to help with the evening "chores," and this left Mr. and Mrs. Bobbsey free to talk when Nan had taken Baby May and the smaller twins out in the yard.

"What do you think we had better do?" asked Mrs. Bobbsey of her husband. "I don't like this shadow of a strange woman always hovering over us and the baby."

"Neither do I. Suppose we go to some other place, and go in such a way—perhaps at night—that she can't find us?"

"I think that would be a good plan. She must have inquired of the neighbors back in Lakeport and so have traced us."

"I suppose so; though I thought we had kept it quiet. But we don't want to spoil the children's summer. I'll look for another place."

The sound of footsteps on the side porch was heard and, looking out, Mrs. Bobbsey saw Nan coming in, followed by Freddie and Flossie.

"You shouldn't come in and leave Baby May out there all alone!" warned Mrs. Bobbsey.

"Oh, she's all right," said Nan. "She's sound asleep, and I can see the carriage from here, and Flossie and Freddie wanted something to eat."

"It's too near supper time," said their mother. "You must wait, my dears," she told the smaller twins. "Don't spoil your appetites."

"I can't spoil mine—it's too big," chuckled Freddie. "I just wanted a cookie."

"So do I," said Flossie.

Their mother finally allowed them a cookie apiece, for she found out that supper would be a bit late, as Mrs. Meekin wanted to finish skimming the milk as she was going to churn the next day.

Then Nan decided she wanted a cookie for herself, so it was perhaps five or ten minutes before the children went back to where they had left Baby May in the carriage.

But, all the while, the carriage was in plain sight from the porch. Even Mr. Bobbsey could watch it, so nothing was feared.

Nan and Flossie and Freddie, munching their molasses cookies, went back to where they had left Baby May, Nan gently raised the coverings to see if May was still asleep.

"Oh! Oh!" she gasped.

"What is it?" Flossie wanted to know.

"Is a bee stinging Baby May?" asked Freddie.

"Oh! Oh, no!" cried Nan, and she was very pale. "Baby May—she—she isn't here! She's gone!"

From the porch Mrs. Bobbsey was watching. She realized that something was wrong, and she ran down to the carriage about which Nan, Flossie and Freddie stood.

"What is it, Nan?" she asked quickly. "Has anything happened?"

"Baby—Baby May!" sobbed Nan. "She's gone! She's been kidnapped!"

CHAPTER XIX

ON THE TRAIL

FLOSSIE, Freddie and Nan were sobbing now. Their tears fell thick and fast and they wailed aloud.

"Children! Children! Be quiet!" ordered Mrs. Bobbsey. "What does it all mean? Baby May can't have been taken. The carriage has been in plain sight all the while. She's probably under the covers, Nan! Don't be silly!"

"I'm not si-si-silly, Mother. Baby May's gone! I—I felt under the covers and she—she isn't there."

"I—I can't feel her to-toes!" sobbed Flossie, her hand in the lower end of the carriage.

By this time Mrs. Bobbsey herself had made sure there was no baby in the carriage. She took out all the coverings.

"She must have tumbled out and crawled

away," she said. "She can't be gone! Look in the grass and bushes, children!"

"Wouldn't she cry if she fell out?" Freddie wanted to know. He had stopped crying when his mother came along.

"She might not cry if she fell on soft leaves and didn't hurt herself," answered Mrs. Bobbsey. "Look carefully, children!"

But all the looking in the world would not have found Baby May just then, and it did not take Mrs. Bobbsey long to make certain that the infant was not around the carriage.

"Well, the worst has happened," she said, and there was the sound of tears in her own voice. "Baby May didn't fall out. She was taken away!"

"I said she was kidnapped!" declared Nan. "Soon as I didn't see her in the carriage and didn't feel her, I knew she was kidnapped! Oh, Mother! what are we going to do? Poor Baby May!"

"I—I want her back!" sobbed Flossie.

"It was that old woman—that old woman with the green umbrella!" exclaimed Freddie. "She took May off, I know she did!"

"I'm beginning to believe so," said Mrs. Bobbsey. "We must do something at once. Call your father, Nan—oh, never mind. Here he comes now!"

Mr. Bobbsey had gone in the house after Nan and the children had departed with their cookies, and now he came out on the porch again. Seeing his wife and the children gathered around the carriage he seemed to guess that something was wrong.

"Has anything happened?" he asked, as he hurried across the grass. "Did May fall out? Why, where is she?" he asked, seeing Nan wheeling the empty carriage.

"Oh, Richard!" sobbed Mrs. Bobbsey, "the little one is gone—kidnapped!"

"No! It isn't possible! Under our very eyes! How could it happen?" Mr. Bobbsey asked.

"I don't know," his wife said. "But she's gone. The old woman must have sneaked up between the time the children left the carriage to get the cookies and the time they went back."

"Then she must have been hiding around

here, waiting for just such a chance," declared Mr. Bobbsey. "This is too much! I must notify the police at once. An alarm must be sent out and we must get on the trail of this person. I believe she is crazy! She ought not to be allowed at large with a baby!"

"Will she—will she hurt Baby May?" asked Flossie, alarmed by her father's excitement.

Then, as his wife made him a signal to be more careful, so as not to frighten the children, Mr. Bobbsey said:

"Oh, no, I don't believe the old woman will hurt May. She must love her a great deal to want to take her away. But anybody who will leave an infant on the steps in a thunder storm shouldn't be allowed to have charge of children. I'll get the police after her at once."

It was one thing to speak about getting the police to work, but it was quite another thing to do this. In the quiet little hamlet of Pine Hill there were no regular police officers—only a constable or two and a justice of the peace.

"But Jim Denton is pretty smart," said Mr. Meekin, when he and his wife had been told of the terrible happening. "I had a horse stolen once, and Jim got it back for me in less than a week. I'll telephone him."

"Say, Dad, can't you and I take the trail after this old woman ourselves?" asked Bert, in a whisper of his father, while Mr. Meekin was at the telephone, calling up the constable.

"Yes, I intend to do what I can," answered Mr. Bobbsey. "I'll take the auto and ride along every road I think the old woman must have taken. And you may go with me, Bert."

"Oh, do you think that will be wise?" asked his wife, overhearing what was said.

"Yes," her husband answered. "Bert will be a help to me. We may have to be gone all night."

Bert's eyes sparkled with pleasure as his father said this. It might be a great adventure!

"Bert, you must take good care of yourself," said his mother anxiously. "I wouldn't have anything happen to you for the world!"

"Oh, I'll be all right, don't worry," returned the son, with all the confidence of a growing boy.

"But that woman may not be as nice as you think. For all we know, she may be crazy and liable to do any wicked thing," remarked Mrs. Meekin.

"I'll keep my eyes open," declared Bert sturdily.

"Jim'll be right over in his car," said Mr. Meekin, as he hung up the telephone. "And while we're waiting, let's look the ground over and see what happened."

"And you must have supper—I'll get it ready right away," said Mrs. Meekin. "Land sakes! To think of such things happening! My goodness!"

She bustled off to get the meal, which was almost ready, and Mr. Bobbsey, with Bert and Mr. Meekin, went to the place where the carriage had been left for just a few minutes alone with Baby May in it. And yet those few minutes were enough for the kidnapping to have taken place.

That it was a kidnapping—and done by the strange old woman in the faded shawl and with the green umbrella—all were now certain. Of course no one had seen her, but everything pointed to her.

"She just waited her chance and then sneaked up," said Bert.

That seemed to have been the manner of it. The back of the carriage was turned toward the house, to keep the sun out of May's eyes as she lay asleep. It would have been an easy matter for the old woman—or any one else—to have sneaked up and taken the baby. She could lift the child, asleep as she was, out of the carriage under the cover of the hood, and the children and Mr. and Mrs. Bobbsey on the porch could not see this take place.

"Well, I can't see anything here," said Mr. Meekin, looking all around the carriage.

"Nor I," agreed Mr. Bobbsey.

"Let's take a look up and down the road," suggested Bert.

But nothing was in sight—no one in view. This was not strange, as there were trees and bushes on either side of the highway, and it would have been an easy matter for the kidnapper to have concealed herself in these for a moment, or longer, and then to have taken some hidden path.

"Well, we must get on the trail at once,"

said Mr. Bobbsey. "You have the police, or whoever does such things, send out a general alarm, Mr. Meekin. Bert and I will start off in our car, and when Jim Denton comes, he can do his part."

"Jim's pretty good," repeated Mr. Meekin. "He got back my horse."

Mrs. Meekin had supper ready in a "jiffy," as she called it. The meal was not quite over when some one was heard running up the side porch. It was some one in a hurry, that was very plain.

CHAPTER XX

AN EXCITING CHASE

THE Bobbsey twins stopped eating and looked one at the other. What could it mean —this hurried rush of some one up the steps? Then Flossie spoke.

"Maybe it's the old woman bringing back Baby May," she whispered.

"If it is, I'm going to catch her!" declared Freddie, getting ready to slip down from his chair.

"Sit still, children," ordered Mrs. Bobbsey.

Bert acted as though, he, too, would like to see who it was, for, as yet, the caller was not in view. But a look from his father kept Bert in his seat. He looked at Nan in a disappointed manner.

"It's Jim Denton," announced Mr. Meekin, as he saw the hurrying visitor through the open door. "Come right in, Jim!" he called. "Had your supper? If you haven't—"

"Oh, I ate long ago," announced the caller, who was the constable, or chief policeman, for Pine Hill. "What's all the excitement about?" he asked. "Have you had another horse stolen, Pete?"

"No, not a horse this time. It's worse—a little baby," said Mr. Meekin. "Didn't they tell you at the post-office, where I telephoned to you?"

"No, they didn't say what it was. Just said something was missing over here and for me to hurry. I did, as soon as I could get a bite to eat. But what do you mean—a baby taken? Is it lost?"

"Worse'n that, Jim," said the farmer. "It's a kidnapping case. You want to do your best on this!"

"I will," promised the constable. "Tell me all about it."

"I'll let Mr. Bobbsey do that," said Mr. Meekin. "It's his baby; or at least he and his wife took care of it. And it was stolen out of the carriage, right in my yard, Jim, with folks on the side porch. Greatest mystery we ever had here! The children left the baby a moment and—"

"Say, I thought you were going to let Mr. Bobbsey tell the story," remarked Jim, with a smile, as he looked at his watch. "If this is a kidnapping case the sooner we get on the trail and chase after the kidnapper the better."

"That's right. You tell him, Mr. Bobbsey," begged Mr. Meekin. "I get so excited thinking about it that my tongue runs away with me."

Then the story was told, the Bobbsey twins telling their share in the sorrowful affair of how Baby May was stolen right out of her carriage, when she was left alone but for a moment.

"Hum!" remarked Constable Jim Denton, when the story was finished. "It is very strange. I'll take a look at the place."

"You won't find any clews there, because we looked," said Bert, with a very grown-up air.

"Well, maybe, I won't. But I'll take a look, just the same," replied the constable.

They all went with him while he looked over the place where the carriage had been left just before Baby May was stolen from it. As

Bert had said, there was little in the way of clews, or anything to tell who the kidnapper was or which way she had gone.

That it was the strange woman with the faded shawl and the green umbrella, every one felt sure.

"I've heard something about that old woman hanging around these parts," the constable said, "but I've never laid eyes on her. This time I hope I do."

"I'm going to help in the search," said Mr. Bobbsey. "My son and I will go off in our auto, but of course we'll act under your orders, Mr. Denton, as you are in charge."

"Well, I don't know that I have any special orders," the constable said slowly. "The main thing is to catch that old woman and get back the baby."

"Oh, yes, I want Baby May back!" sighed Mrs. Bobbsey.

"And I want her, too," said Flossie, with tears in her eyes.

"Have you an automobile, Mr. Denton?" asked the father of the Bobbsey twins.

"Well, some folks call it that, and then

again they speak of it as a tin Lizzie," chuckled the constable. "It gets me where I want to go and back again. Well, we'd better start if we're going," he added.

"That's what I think," agreed Mr. Bobbsey. "And as there is no telling which way this old woman has gone, one of us can go up the main road, and the other down the main road until we get some sort of clew."

"A good idea," said the constable. "It ought not to be hard to find this old woman. Traveling with a baby, as she is, some one is bound to take notice of her. It'll be an easier case than your lost horse, Pete," he said to Mr. Meekin.

"I'm sure I hope so," said Mrs. Meekin, who had learned to love Baby May, as had every one else.

After arranging to telephone in as soon as he should have any news, Constable Jim Denton went off in his little automobile, going up the road, or toward the next town of Rosemount.

"Well, Bert, I guess we'd better start on our

part of the chase," said Mr. Bobbsey to his son.

"Do you think it safe to take Bert with you?" asked Mrs. Bobbsey.

"Why not?" asked her husband.

"Oh, Mother, I want to go!" pleaded Bert. "Crickity grasshoppers—"

"But your father may be on the road all night—or at least away all night, my dear."

"I can stay up all night, Mother!" insisted Bert.

"He'll be all right," said Mr. Bobbsey, with a smile. "And I may need him to help me. We sha'n't travel quite all night. If we get too far away to return by, say, eleven o'clock, we'll stay at a hotel all night. Don't worry, Mother!"

He kissed his wife good-bye, and kissed Nan, Flossie and Freddie.

"I'll bring back Baby May!" said Bert firmly, as he, too, kissed his mother.

"I'm sure I hope so," murmured Mrs. Bobbsey.

Mr. Bobbsey and Bert took the "down road," as it was called, leading to the city of Millville, 'though the city itself was several miles away. However, there were small towns and villages in between, and it was thought that some news might be obtained in one of these of the old woman and Baby May.

"Maybe she might go off into the woods and camp there, like a gypsy," suggested Bert, as he and his father started off in the automobile.

"No, I hardly think so," replied Mr. Bobbsey. "A little baby like May would not fare very well if kept out all night in a camp in the woods—that is, unless the woman had a tent, and I don't believe she has that."

"But where has she been staying all the while she's been spying on us and trying to get the baby back?" asked Bert.

"That's what I can't find out," said his father. "She must have lived somewhere around here, and yet we can't get a trace of her. If she boarded with any of the farmers we would have heard about it."

"Maybe she found an old hut or cabin, and is staying in that," said Bert.

"Perhaps," his father admitted. "Well,

we'll inquire all along as we go, and we may find her."

They stopped at the first house they passed after leaving the home of Mr. Meekin. But the people there had not seen a woman and baby going past. They asked all sorts of questions, wanting to know all about the kidnapping, but Mr. Bobbsey did not have time to say much. As soon as he found out they could tell him nothing he hurried on with Bert.

It was the same at the next half dozen houses they stopped at—no one had seen the kidnapper.

"But we must keep on with the search," said Mr. Bobbsey.

"Of course," agreed Bert. "I want to get back Baby May!"

CHAPTER XXI

IN THE DUCK POND

MEANWHILE, back in the house at Pine Hill, the other Bobbsey children and their mother waited anxiously for news from Bert and his father.

At first Nan was sure the two would come back in an hour after setting off, bringing back Baby May. But when the long hand of the clock had gone slowly all around the face twice, making two hours, Nan sighed and said:

"I guess it's going to take longer than I thought."

"I'm afraid so," agreed her mother.

Flossie and Freddie, however, though just as anxious to get back Baby May as were Bert and Nan, did not think so much about the kidnapping of the little one. Flossie and Freddie liked to have fun all the while, and just waiting for some one to come back was not much fun.

"Let's do something," proposed Freddie, after a while.

"All right," agreed Flossie. "What'll we do?"

Freddie thought for a few moments. Then he said:

"Let's go wading in the pond."

"Oh-o-o-oo!" exclaimed Flossie, her eyes opening wide in surprise. "Mother said we mustn't go there!" she added.

"That was yesterday," said Freddie, with a shake of his curly head. "Yesterday it looked like it was going to rain, and she told us not to go to the pond. To-day it isn't going to rain, so we can go to the pond and wade—with our shoes and stockings off," he went on, after another thought.

"Are you sure?" asked Flossie.

"Course I'm sure," answered Freddie. "Come on!"

Perhaps if Flossie had not wanted so much to go and wade in the pond she might have thought more of what her mother had said the

day before. This was that neither she nor
Freddie was to go in wading. But then Freddie might be right. Mrs. Bobbsey might not
have wanted the children to play in the water
when it was likely to rain.

Now the sun was shining and the water of
the pond sparkled in the bright light. The
pond was out of sight of the house. It was
a place where a brook widened out, making
a swimming space for the ducks. Flossie and
Freddie had been allowed to sail toy boats on
it, but had not been allowed to go in wading.

"It's too muddy," Mrs. Bobbsey had said.

But now the two little Bobbsey twins made
their way down to this pond, no one in the
house seeing them.

"I'll get my shoes and stockings off before
you do!" cried Freddie, sitting down on the
ground near the water.

"You will not! I can beat you!" cried
Flossie.

She did, but she tore one of her stockings
while taking it off in such a hurry.

"I beat! I beat!" she cried, dancing up and
down.

"But you tore your stocking!" cried Freddie, pointing to the hole.

"I don't care—it was an old stocking," replied Flossie.

"Well, anyhow, I'll get in wading first!" shouted Freddie. He made a dash toward the water, Flossie following closely after him.

"Oh! Oh!" suddenly cried the little girl.

Freddie turned and saw that she had fallen down.

"Did you hurt yourself, Flossie?" asked her brother kindly.

"N-n-no; not mu-mu-much!" she stammered. "Is my—now, is my nose red?" she asked, raising her head from the ground, where she still lay.

Freddie ran forward and dipped one foot in the water of the pond.

"That's to show I beat and got in first," he said. Then he went back to Flossie who was still stretched out on the ground. He wanted to be kind to his sister, but a race was a race. "Your nose is a little red," he went on.

"Is it bleeding?" Flossie wanted to know, about ready to cry.

"No, it isn't bleeding," Freddie answered.

"Then I guess it's all right," Flossie went on. "Please help me up, Freddie."

Freddie did this, and the two barefooted Bobbsey twins, hand in hand, walked toward the pond. Freddie did not care now if Flossie got in ahead of him, for he had wet his feet first.

However, Flossie was a bit timid, so she stood on the edge of the pond and said:

"Wade in again, Freddie, and tell me if it's very deep and if it's cold."

"It isn't deep and it isn't cold," declared Freddie. "I'll show you, Flossie!"

He waded boldly out into the pond, splashing about and getting the bottoms of his little trousers wet. He turned toward Flossie, to tell her to come on out, but, suddenly, a queer look came over the little boy's face.

"Oh, Flossie!" he cried. "Something's got me by the toe! Oh, I guess it's a mud turkle! Go call mother!"

Flossie paused for a moment on the edge of the pond.

"Go on! Go on!" cried Freddie, dancing

about with one foot out of the water. The other seemed stuck in the mud. "Go on. Call mother! Tell her a mud turkle has me by the toe!"

"I don't see any turkle," remarked Flossie. Both she and Freddie called it "turkle," instead of turtle.

"Well, the turkle is here all right!" Freddie exclaimed. "He has me by the toe! Maybe it's a snapping turkle 'stid of a mud turkle! But go call mother!"

Away ran Flossie, and she was soon gasping to her mother:

"It's got him by the toe! It's got him by the toe!"

"What has who by the toe?" asked Mrs. Bobbsey.

"The turkle has Freddie by the toe," explained Flossie. "Come on, Mother!"

"Where is Freddie?" asked his mother.

"Down in the duck pond," answered Flossie.

"Didn't I tell you not to go wading there?" exclaimed Mrs. Bobbsey. But she did not wait for Flossie to answer. On hurried the mother, of the Bobbsey twins, Flossie keeping alongside of her.

"Freddie said it was all right to go in wading to-day, 'cause it was yesterday you said we couldn't go in," remarked Flossie.

"Oh, my goodness!" gasped Mrs. Bobbsey. "Such children!"

By this time she was within sight of the pond where Freddie stood near the edge. He was crying and was splashed from head to foot with muddy water.

"Oh, Freddie! Are you hurt, child?" called his mother.

"The—the turkle's—got hold of my toe yet and he won't let go!" Freddie sobbed.

There was a plank on the edge of the pond, and, pushing this out into the water, Mrs. Bobbsey stepped on it until she could reach the little boy without getting her own feet wet. She put her arms around Freddie and lifted him from the water. That is, she tried to lift him, but at first he did not come.

"He's stuck in the mud!" shouted Flossie.

"It's my foot! The turkle has hold of it!" screamed Freddie.

"It must be a very large turtle!" gasped Mrs. Bobbsey. But she did not really believe that a turtle had hold of the little boy's foot, though he certainly was held fast.

She gave another pull, and this time Freddie came up in her arms. Something was dangling from one foot. At the sight of it Flossie, on the bank, set up a shout.

"Oh, it isn't a turkle after all!" cried the little girl. "It's a big jug!"

And so it was. Freddie, wading about in the pond, had stuck his big toe in the mouth of a brown jug that some one had thrown into the duck pond. The jug had stuck to the little boy's foot, and to him it seemed exactly as if a "turkle" had him.

As Mrs. Bobbsey raised Freddie up in her arms, the jug fell from his toe and splashed back into the pond.

"There goes your turtle," said his mother. "My! what a time you've had! You shouldn't have gone in wading, Flossie and Freddie!"

"I told him you said not to," remarked the little girl.

"But I didn't think you meant to-day," observed Freddie, as he sat down on the grass and looked carefully at his big toe. Aside from being red, like Flossie's nose, it was not cut or hurt.

"I didn't want you to go in wading any time in this pond," said the children's mother. "There is broken glass in it and pieces of tin on which you might cut your feet. That's why I wanted you to stay out."

"Oh!" murmured Freddie. "I thought it was 'cause you didn't want us to get wet."

"Don't go in again!" warned Mrs. Bobbsey, and thinking Freddie had been frightened enough she did not punish him any more.

"I—I tore my stocking a little," confessed Flossie, wanting to have all the unpleasant things over with at once.

"That's too bad," said her mother. "You should have minded me. Well, put on your shoes and we'll go back to the house."

One might have thought this would be the last of the adventures of Flossie and Freddie for that day, but it was not. Just before sunset they went out in the barn to play in the hay. They slid on the sweet-smelling dried grass for a time, coasting down from the mow to the barn floor.

Then Flossie had an idea.

"Let's hunt where the hens lay their eggs and bring in some," proposed the little girl.

"That'll be fun," agreed Freddie.

They crawled about in the hay, looking here and there for nests with white eggs in them. Suddenly Flossie gave a cry as she felt herself slipping on the smooth hay into a hole.

"What's the matter?" asked Freddie, who was in another part of the barn. "Did you find a nest?"

Flossie answered "yes," for she had found a nest. She had slid right into one containing nearly a dozen eggs. She had sat down on them, smashing the eggs and covering herself with broken shells and sticky whites and yellows.

"Oh, you'd better call mother!" sighed Flossie, when she saw what had happened.

"This is worser than when the jug-turkle caught me by the toe!" shouted Freddie, as he dashed for the house.

"Oh, my goodness, what will happen next?"

sighed Mrs. Bobbsey, when she saw the woeful sight of Flossie, very dirty, sitting in the nest, for right there the little girl had stayed, waiting for her mother to come to her. She took the little girl into the house to clean her, and when Flossie had on dry clothes her mother said:

"Now you and Freddie stay on the porch until bedtime."

"Do you think Daddy and Bert will come back soon?" asked Freddie.

"Perhaps," said their mother. "At any rate, I hope so."

CHAPTER XXII

CAUGHT AT LAST

MEANWHILE Bert and his father were keeping on with the search for Baby May. Once they saw an old woman going along the road ahead of them, carrying a sack over her back.

"Oh, maybe she has Baby May in that bag!" cried Bert.

His father hardly thought so, but speeded up the auto until they reached the old woman.

"What do you want?" she demanded.

"Have you a baby in that sack?" asked Mr. Bobbsey.

"Goodness, no! I should hope not," answered the woman, with a laugh. "I've got potatoes in here. Why would I be carrying a baby?"

Then Mr. Bobbsey explained that he and Bert were looking for a kidnapper and they inquired of the "potato woman," as they called her, whether she had seen anything of Baby May.

"No, I haven't," she answered. "I've just been after these potatoes, that's all."

As the bag was heavy, Mr. Bobbsey gave the woman and her potatoes a ride to the woman's house.

"Thank you," she said, as she got down. "I hope you find that kidnapper and the baby."

"We may get some news of her in the morning," said Mr. Bobbsey, for it was now getting on toward night.

The two in the automobile kept on to the next town where Mr. Bobbsey had decided to stay all night. There was little use in going farther, and they could get no news of the strange woman by inquiring at the post-office and the stores.

Bert and his father went to the one hotel in the place, and from there they telephoned back to Mrs. Bobbsey at Pine Hill, telling her their plans.

"I don't suppose you have any news, have

you?" asked Mr. Bobbsey of his wife over the wire. "Did Jim Denton get any clews?"

"Yes," she answered. "He found some persons who had seen the old woman, carrying a bundle, going down the road. That was the baby, I'm sure. But Jim lost trace of the woman. Very likely she got a ride in some auto. But he's going to keep right on with the search."

"If she went down his part of the road, then there isn't much use in our keeping on this way," said Mr. Bobbsey. "Bert and I will return in the morning."

So it was decided. Bert was rather sorry his adventure had come to such an end, for he hoped they might get some trace of the strange woman in the direction he and his father had taken, but it was not to be.

In the morning Mr. Bobbsey and Bert went back to Pine Hill, reaching there about ten o'clock. Soon after they arrived they had a telephone message from Mr. Denton.

"The old woman was seen around the town of Cardley," the constable said. "You'd better go over there, and I'll meet you. I don't know her and I might make a mistake and pick out the wrong one."

"I'll know that old woman again, if I see her!" exclaimed Bert.

"And I'll know Baby May," added his father.

"Oh, can't I go with you?" begged Nan, as her father and brother were about to start off again.

"You might take her with you," suggested Mrs. Bobbsey. "If you do get Baby May back Nan can take care of her."

So Nan was allowed to go. Flossie and Freddie cried and begged to go also, but this was not permitted. However, their mother promised to take them on a picnic to pass the time until the others should return.

Constable Jim Denton proved to be a good detective. He had finally got trace of the old woman carrying the baby, and he found that, as had been thought, she had been given a ride—a "lift," the constable called it—by a kind farmer.

"He left her in Cardley, and she said she

was going to stay there all night," Mr. Denton explained.

Mr. Bobbsey made good speed to Cardley and found the constable there waiting for him.

"Where is the old woman?" asked Mr. Bobbsey, as he met the constable at the village hotel.

"She's stopping at a farmhouse just outside the town," he said. "I located her, but I didn't want to make any move to arrest her, for fear she'd get excited and maybe hurt the baby, or steal off again. She's pretty well tired out, from what I hear, and I guess it will be an easy matter to catch her."

"Is Baby May all right?" Nan asked anxiously.

"Oh, bless your heart, yes!" replied Mr. Denton. "I guess the old woman took good care of the baby."

They all went out to the farmhouse in Mr. Bobbsey's automobile, as the constable said his little car had a flat tire. As they approached the place Nan and Bert saw, standing out in the front yard, a figure they well knew.

It was that of the strange old woman they had first seen passing their house and later sneaking around Pine Hill. As soon as the woman, who was without her shawl now and who did not have an umbrella, saw them, she made a dash toward the house.

But Jim Denton was too quick for her. Leaping from the automobile while it was still moving, he caught her by the arm and cried:

"No, you don't! We have you now! You can't get away with the baby again!"

The old woman did not struggle. Indeed, now that she was caught, she seemed very calm and not at all queer.

"Very well," she said. "I am not going to run away. You will find everything all right. I have a very good claim to this baby."

"That you'll have to explain to the police," said Mr. Bobbsey, in a stern voice. "Where is Baby May?"

"Her name isn't May. It's Jenny," returned the old woman, with a faint smile. "Jenny Watson. If you'll come in I'll explain everything."

Wonderingly the two Bobbsey twins

followed their father, the constable and the old woman into the farmhouse. The old woman suddenly burst into tears as she was about to open the door of a room.

"I hope nothing has happened to Baby May," said Mr. Bobbsey, for he and his wife had grown to love the baby very much.

"Oh, no, Jenny is all right. She is asleep, I think," said the old woman. "But I feel so bad over all that has happened. It wasn't exactly my fault—I couldn't help it. But if I had not gotten the baby back! Oh, it would have been terrible!" She wiped away her tears.

"Don't feel bad," said Mr. Bobbsey kindly. "Of course I don't understand it at all—why you should abandon the baby and then kidnap her—but—"

"Hush!" whispered the old lady, putting her finger to her lips as she stepped into the darkened room. Softly she raised the curtain, and there on a bed Nan and the others saw the baby sweetly sleeping.

"Oh, the little darling!" murmured Nan. "I'm so glad we have her back!"

"Well, my dear," whispered the old woman, "I'm afraid I can't let you have her back. You see she has a father and mother of her own, and they will want their baby."

"Then you aren't the mother?" asked Mr. Bobbsey, more and more puzzled over the matter.

"No, I am not Jenny's mother," was the answer. "If you will come into the next room, where we can talk without waking baby, I'll tell you the story. It is a very strange one."

"Well," said Mr. Bobbsey, when they were all seated in a pleasant room of the farmhouse where, the old woman said, she had engaged board for herself and the baby, "we are now ready for the story. And then I must telephone to my wife that the baby is all right."

"Your wife took very good care of Jenny, and I want to thank her when I see her," said the old woman. "Now I will be as short as I can.

"My name," she said, "is Sarah Martin. I have been a widow for a number of years. Several months ago my cousin, Mrs. Henry

Watson, came to me and said her husband had to go to South America on a business trip, and she felt that she ought to go with him, as he was not in very good health.

"They did not think it would be safe to take the baby to South America with them, so I agreed to look after little Jenny—that's her real name—Jenny Watson."

"We called her May Washington Bobbsey," said Bert.

"We did that," explained his father, "because we found her on the first day of May, and we understood from the railroad men that you had given a name that sounded like Washington."

"Wassingham was my name before I was married," explained Mrs. Martin. "Very likely I gave that name when I was out of my mind—partly crazy, I guess I must have been —and they understood me to say Washington."

"Was that on account of the baby?" asked the constable.

"No, not exactly. But the fact that I had lost Jenny made me feel worse," replied Mrs. Martin. "Well, as I was telling you, my cousin and her husband went to South America and left Jenny with me. They were to be gone about six months, and they are now on their way home. If I hadn't been able to get Jenny for them before they arrived, I don't know what I would have done!

"Everything went along nicely for the first month. I kept Jenny with me in my home at Blakeville, and she grew and thrived. Then, one day, when I was cleaning a closet, some dishes fell on my head. I was knocked unconscious, and when I was able to get up I had a queer feeling. I wasn't myself. I seemed to have forgotten my name, and all I could remember about the baby was a feeling that I ought to get rid of her.

"So, not really knowing what I was doing, I put her in a basket, wrapped a shawl around myself, and, taking a green umbrella, I set out. I had only one idea in mind—to leave the baby at some house where there were other children. I must have felt that in such a place she would be well taken care of.

"I took the train from my home to your town, though I don't remember anything about getting off the train. I do remember, though, tramping around in the rain. I saw some children's faces at a window, and I made up my mind that would be a good house at which to leave the baby."

"That was our house," murmured Nan.

"Yes, dearie, that must have been your house," said Mrs. Martin. "Well, once I had picked out the house, I lingered around until after dark, and then, making sure the baby was well protected in the basket, I left her on your doorstep and, ringing the bell, slipped off in the rain and darkness. I hid myself and watched to see if the door would be opened, and when it wasn't, I went softly up again and rang the bell a second time."

"We thought it was the lightning making the bell ring," explained Bert, "for we couldn't see any one on the steps."

"No, I slipped away as soon as I rang the bell, and I suppose you didn't notice the basket in the darkness," said Mrs. Martin. "But after I had rung the bell the second time I felt sure you would take in the baby, so I slipped away for good.

"What happened for several weeks after that, I don't remember. But finally some one noticed that I was acting queerly, and I was taken to a hospital, and there I was cured. Then when I remembered what I had done— taken Baby Jenny away and deserted her—I went nearly crazy again. I tried to remember where I had left her, but for a long time I couldn't. Then, when I did get to your house, I watched my chance to take the baby away again."

"Why didn't you come in and tell us your story?" asked Mr. Bobbsey. "We would have given you back the baby had we known."

"I was afraid you wouldn't believe me," answered Mrs. Martin. "So I watched my chance. I managed to find out that you had gone to Pine Hill, and I followed you there. Then I kept on waiting for an opportunity to take back the baby, as I had a right to do. At last, yesterday, my chance came. I saw Baby Jenny asleep in her carriage, I slipped up and took her out. Then I slipped away, hiding in the woods until after dark, and getting a ride until I reached this place.

"I thought everything would be all right and that I could restore the baby to her parents, who are expected home in a few days. But when I saw you coming I feared you would take her away from me again, so I rushed in here. Then I decided to tell you the whole story. I knew I had a right to the baby, now that my mind is well again."

"Of course you have a right to the baby until her parents come," said Mr. Bobbsey. "It has been a queer mix-up all around, and I am very sorry for you. Have you written to Mr. and Mrs. Watson?"

"I didn't write and tell them I had lost the baby," answered Mrs. Martin. "I didn't dare do that. But I had a cablegram from them asking how Jenny was, and to-day I sent them a message, saying she was well. For indeed she is. Your wife took very good care of her. Oh, I am so sorry for all the trouble I have caused," and the old woman wept again.

"You couldn't help it," said Mr. Bobbsey kindly. "Perhaps you had better come back and stay with my wife until Mr. and Mrs.

Watson arrive from South America. Bring Baby Jenny and stay with us."

"Oh, yes, please do!" begged Nan. "We won't know what to do without Baby May—I mean Baby Jenny!" she quickly corrected herself.

"All right, I'll do that," said Mrs. Martin.

The children were very excited and began making plans for taking care of the infant. They were to get good practise for their next adventure to be known as "The Bobbsey Twins Keeping House."

Before going to the farm, they telephoned the news to Mrs. Bobbsey at Pine Hill, and there was a happy meeting when, once more, the baby was with those who had cared for the little foundling.

"You poor woman! How you must have suffered," said Mrs. Bobbsey to Mrs. Martin, after having heard the story.

"You will never know how terrible it was when I realized that I had given the baby away —left her on a strange doorstep. And then I couldn't remember for a long while where it was!" said Mrs. Martin. "But now it has all ended happily."

And so it had, for a few days later the ship bearing Mr. and Mrs. Watson came in from South America, and the parents made a quick trip out to Pine Hill, where the mother gathered into her arms the baby who had gone through so many strange adventures.

No one blamed Mrs. Martin, for it was an accident, though undoubtedly if she had come to the Bobbseys and explained everything, instead of trying to kidnap the baby, it would have been much better. But, as she said, she hardly knew what she was doing.

"Well, I wish we could keep the baby," said Nan. "But maybe something else will happen pretty soon."

"Maybe," agreed Bert. "Anyhow, it was exciting while it lasted." And the other Bobbsey twins agreed with this.

THE END

THE
BOBBSEY TWINS BOOKS

by Laura Lee Hope

These are books that charm boys and girls between the ages of three and ten. Many of the adventures of these famous twins are comical in the extreme, and all the accidents and incidents that ordinarily happen to youthful personages happen to these many-sided little mortals.

THE BOBBSEY TWINS

GROSSET & DUNLAP

Publishers   NEW YORK

THE
HONEY BUNCH BOOKS
by Helen Louise Thorndyke

Honey Bunch is a dainty, thoughtful little girl, and to know her is to take her to your heart at once. Little girls everywhere will want to discover what interesting experiences she is having wherever she goes.

HONEY BUNCH:

GROSSET & DUNLAP

Publishers   NEW YORK

Stories of Fun and Friendship

THE MAIDA BOOKS
by INEZ HAYNES IRWIN

MAIDA'S LITTLE SHOP

In a darling little shop of her own Maida makes many
iends with the school children who buy her fascinating
ares.

MAIDA'S LITTLE HOUSE

All of her friends spend a happy summer in Maida's perfect
ttle house that has everything a child could wish for.

MAIDA'S LITTLE SCHOOL

Three delightful grownups come to visit and the children
tudy many subjects without knowing that they are really
going to school."

MAIDA'S LITTLE ISLAND

Great is the joy of the Big Eight when Maida's father takes
hem for a vacation to *Spectacles*, where exploring the island
provides endless fun and many thrilling adventures.

MAIDA'S LITTLE CAMP

High in the Adirondacks the four boys and four girls of the
Big Eight spend a glorious month of fun and discovery.

GROSSET & DUNLAP : *Publishers* : NEW YORK

THE
LITTLE INDIAN SERIE

by David Cory

The beauty of Indian legend — the thrill
Indian adventure — the poetry of the Indian
religion, and, above all, the sturdy manhood a
the idealism of the Indian boy will be an inspi
tion to every child.

LITTLE INDIAN

WHITE OTTER

RED FEATHER

STAR MAIDEN

LONE STAR

RAVEN WING

HAWK EYE

CHIPPEWA TRAIL

GROSSET & DUNLAP

Publishers   New Yor